Runa

CU00864305

Sally Clements

This is a work of fiction. Names, characters, places and incidents are the product of the author's imagination or are used fictiously, and any resemblance to actual persons living or dead, business establishments, events, or locales, is entirely coincidental.

Runaway Groom

ISBN-13: 978-1489530325
ISBN-10: 1489530320

Dedication

For Fifi and Anton

Chapter One

This time, everything will be perfect.

April Leigh laid out swatches of slippery silk and gleaming duchess-satin on the smooth wooden worktop. The wedding dress sketch she'd worked on tirelessly over the past week was propped up on the wooden easel, and the rest of her collection had been tidied onto the hanging rails opposite the full-length windows that bled light into her studio space. Now all she needed was the bride.

She pushed back the sleeve of her heavy black sweater and checked her wafer-thin black watch. June should be here. Rising from her chair, she refilled her coffee cup and gazed from the window onto the bustling street below. The intercom buzzed.

"It's me!"

"Come on up." Warmth filled April at the thought of seeing her sister again. It had been too long.

She swung the door open wide, heart pounding as the elevator juddered to a halt. Her sister's form was visible through the cage, and as April stepped forward, June slid the door sideways, compressing it into a metal lattice pleat.

"Hey, you." Instantly they were in each other's arms,

June's familiar feel and smell jerking April back in time. Even when she was a teenager June had never been too cool to shown affection for her younger sister. Her open and outgoing nature hadn't ever been constrained or dented— by anything. She'd even risen above the event that would have crushed a lesser woman.

She was April's hero.

Now, at last, she'd have her happy ever after. The fact she'd asked April to contribute to her special day was the cherry-on-top.

"Come on in."

"Wow, this place is amazing." June gazed around the huge room.

June still lived in Ireland. This was the first time she'd visited the new London apartment April had moved into once she left college.

"Well, it's a lot better than the last place. The bedsit was so tiny I couldn't actually have more than one person in it at a time, unless they wanted to stand on the coffee table. It's close to work too." April grinned. Her place of work, The Coffee Haven, was directly below her apartment. Working there was pretty much the perfect job—anything to do with coffee had to be a perfect job to a caffeine addict. When her boss, Elizabeth, had confided she was moving from the large open-plan studio apartment and moving to the suburbs, it felt as though the planets had aligned perfectly.

Elizabeth had been delighted to find a tenant she knew and trusted, and April's boss had become her landlady.

"It's mostly one big room, with a small bedroom and bathroom at the end." April waved an arm around. "When Elizabeth lived here, she had more furniture, and this was the open-plan sitting room and kitchen. I shifted the sofa closer to the fireplace, and filled the rest of the space with my…"

June looked around. "Your work stuff."

"Yes." Everything had its place. A large table held her sewing machine. Her computer sat in the middle of the desk in the corner. Bolts of material were stacked on shelves. There was even a stand holding all of her threads, sequins and beads, carefully placed in the perfect position so she could grab them in a flash.

The apartment could do with some homey touches, some throws or rugs to soften the acres of wooden floor but those would come in time.

Right now, her meager funds were stretched to the limit paying the rent and keeping the lights on. All she needed was a place to work. And with its floor to ceiling expanse of glass letting in lots of natural light, this place was pretty darned perfect.

"You didn't get lost on the tube?"

June grinned. "Not with these directions. That was the longest text I've ever seen in my life. Your fingertips must have melted."

"I typed it a while ago. I have it saved in drafts." The route to her apartment on the outskirts of London was a fairly direct one, with only a couple of changes of train on the underground, but to make it easy she'd written out step-by-step instructions to text to the terminally disorganized.

April eyed June's bag. "What have you brought?"

"Pictures." She put the bag on the coffee table. "More wedding magazines."

The rails holding dresses caught June's attention. "Wow, these are great, is this it?"

"Yup." No-one had seen the new collection yet. Having her sister examine the designs for her very first fashion show set a flutter of butterflies loose in April's stomach.

"All black?" June's fingers flicked through the dresses.

"All black," April confirmed. "But I've used a variety of different fabrics in each one."

June pulled one of the dresses from the rack. "Oh, I see what you mean. This one is gorgeous. I love the way you've done the inlay at the front." The black damask dress had a panel of sheer black sewn in which would reveal the wearer's cleavage. "It's tiny." She held it up against her figure.

"All the designers are using the same models. They're all slender and tall."

"So when is the show, and can I come?"

"It's on the 24th of March." April squeezed her hands together into fists, then stretched her fingers out again. "I have the collection made, but I still have to decide on their hair, makeup and accessories."

June patted her back. "You'll be fine. You're always so well organized. Look at you, you've already made all the dresses! How many designers are showing a collection?"

"There are four of us. I couldn't believe it when they asked me to join them, the other three are all established, and I've only just qualified."

"Your work is fantastic. I'm convinced you're going to be a big star. This is just the beginning, next year you'll be at London Fashion week, and in all the newspapers. I'm so proud of you, April. And just think—I'm going to be your very first bride!"

April swallowed. "I wanted to ask you something."

"Out with it, then." June flicked back her long blonde hair.

"I wanted to ask you if you'd wear your wedding dress on the catwalk." The image of June wearing a beautiful ivory wedding dress as the finale of April's show had come to her in a dream. Having a totally black collection was edgy and unusual, and one perfect white wedding dress at the end would be a perfect counterpoint.

"I…" June's eyes widened. "I'd love to!" She hugged April close, then pulled back. "But won't I look huge? I'm no waif."

"You'll look beautiful." Encased in a dress made for her, with her blonde long hair pinned up and accessorized with pearl clips, June would make the perfect bride. "Come and look at the design I've drawn for the dress."

June had very specific ideas which April had worked into the design. The dress would be A-line, with a sweetheart neckline, and fitted with a natural waist. June's shoulders were shapely, and she had a killer cleavage, so they'd decided the dress should be strapless.

"I've added pearl detailing here on the bodice," April explained, tracing the drawing with a finger. "And the choice of material will determine if the dress is very formal or floatier, we could attach an overlay in a different fabric if you want."

She moved to the fabric samples on the table. "This is duchess-satin, which is very lush but also quite thick and stiff. If you want something with more movement, the heavy silk is good."

June picked up the duchess satin. "I love this. It's sexy, isn't it?"

April nodded.

"The color though…" June frowned.

The samples were both ivory. "You could go with a

creamier color, rather than the white, the pearls come in a variety of shades to match."

June pulled a stack of wedding magazines from her bag. She flicked through one, then stabbed the page with a red-tipped finger. "I was thinking of maybe going with a color, rather than just white. What do you think?"

April blinked. The dresses in the pictures ranged in color from blood red through shades of mocha and coffee, to metallic shades of silver and bronze. She'd never, for one moment, considered that June might want a dress in anything other than virginal white. This wedding was such a miracle; a second chance at happy-ever-after all of them had feared might never happen. She'd thought June would want to do the whole traditional bride thing.

"What color were you thinking?"

"Well the red is a bit over the top, I'm pretty sure Michael's family would have a complete fit." She grinned. "The wedding is going to be all over the American society pages. It can't help but be, with his father in politics. But I love the silver and grey dresses, don't you?"

June was a woman of the world. The days of a bride wearing a white dress to telegraph her chastity were outdated, but the thought that June had been influenced by her past angered April. "Do you not want to wear white because of—you know…"

June's lips pressed together. "Because of the last time I was going to be married?" She walked to the window and stared out. "I didn't want to wear white then either. And seven years ago, wearing a colored dress would have been scandalous." She turned back. "And I got to be scandalous before I'd even thought about dresses."

April walked over and slung an arm around her sister's

shoulders. "It wasn't your fault. You weren't the one to call it all off."

"Yes, but I was the pregnant teenager, wasn't I?" There was a trace of sadness in her smile. "For a while anyway."

They hadn't spoken of June's previous engagement for years. She'd been barely eighteen when she became pregnant, and once the pregnancy was confirmed, her boyfriend Matthew Logan had proposed. When she'd miscarried in the first month, April had naively presumed they'd go ahead with the wedding anyway. Matthew was a constant visitor to the house, and had seemed devoted to June, even though they were both still at school.

Looking back, it was difficult to tell who was more shocked that he'd run.

"I'm so lucky to have Michael," June murmured. "I love him more than I ever thought I could love someone."

June had been wasted on a man who didn't even have the decency to stick around. April squeezed her lips together. In the seven years since, June had made a new life for herself, and was even being so brave as to trust again. As for Matthew, who knew where he'd ended up?

June pointed at the page. "I like the grey and the silver ones. What do you think?"

The grey wedding dress was undoubtedly beautiful, but the silver... "I love the silver. You'll look like a princess in silver." A princess inside and out. April flicked open the brochure of pearls. "And we could use this shade of pearls as accents. I'll get some samples of different fabrics in silver and grey this week. How long are you and Michael in London for?"

"His parents are flying in on Wednesday and staying for a week then we're flying to Ireland to introduce them to

Mum and then out to Spain to meet Dad and Inez. I hope they all get on. I'm really nervous."

There was no way Michael's parents could avoid falling in love with June, just as their son had. April squeezed June's hand.

June's eyes clouded. "I know the thought of the wedding has brought back memories for everyone. Mum's mentioned the past a few times."

"Does Michael..." April's mouth was dry. "Does he know?"

"About Matthew?" June's smile held a hint of sadness. "Yes, I told him before he proposed. I reckoned someone would tell him at some stage, and it might as well be me."

"I wonder what happened to Matthew." The words were out before April's brain could communicate with her mouth and stop them. "Oh, I'm sorry, I..."

"Matthew's living and working in London." June walked over and poured a cup of coffee.

It was as though a fog had descended. April heard June's words, but couldn't make sense of them. She shook her head and rubbed her eyes. "You've kept in contact?"

"Not exactly, but I know where he is." June turned. Her gaze locked with April's. "He's not a bad man, you know. We were very young. I'm glad we never married. We would have made each other unhappy, sooner or later. Now I have Michael—I'm so happy. I wish Matthew nothing but the best."

"You can't possibly mean that." April crossed her arms. "You're a very generous person, but he doesn't deserve your forgiveness, never mind your good wishes. I hope I never see him again for as long as I live. Not everyone deserves a second chance."

An errant memory nagged at her. Years ago, she'd greeted Matthew's arrival at their house with almost as much enthusiasm as June. Back in school, she'd nursed a crush on her friend Amy's older brother. The entire Logan clan were so charismatic and good-looking, it was difficult not to. Of course, she'd been a sixteen year old kid—a teenager with a mouthful of braces that made her self-conscious.

In Matthew's company, her heart sped up and she became totally tongue-tied and awkward. With his intense navy blue eyes, and almost-black hair tumbling across his forehead, he'd been every teenager's fantasy. She'd tried to hide her attraction, and he'd seemed oblivious to her crush. He'd been kind, been fun. Back then, she'd dreamed of one day finding a man just like him.

"Do you ever see Amy?" It was as though June had zoned in on April's thoughts.

She shook her head. Their friendship had hit the skids pretty much immediately after their siblings' relationship. *I guess in a warzone you pick a side.*

June tilted her head to the side. "Are you seeing anyone?" Her eyebrows rose.

"No. Well, not really." She'd gone on a couple of dates recently with another barista, or should that be baristo? Joshua was nice, uncomplicated, but didn't exactly set her on fire. He'd tried, but the lack of chemistry was obvious.

"Might you bring someone to the wedding?"

"Are you kidding? Bringing someone to your wedding would be disastrous. Dad would have me married off before I'd even completed the introductions."

June sat on the sofa and patted the seat next to her. She had a familiar look on her face, the one that usually meant that she was going to ask a favor April wasn't going to enjoy giving.

On stiff legs April walked over and sat down.

June placed her soft, manicured hand over April's clenched hands. "In that case, I need another favor. I want you to look after Matthew at the wedding."

*****

Matthew Logan breathed in the clear crisp air and looked up into a cloudless sky. Conditions were perfect.

"Thank you all for coming today." He smiled at the employees who had answered his call for volunteers, all clad in their running gear. It was strange to see them in out of their usual suits and professional work wear. "I really appreciate you guys helping us out here, and for bringing your supporters along. Let me explain how this is going to work."

The abandoned airfield outside London still had its uses, mostly as a training road for learner drivers, but today—today the quiet track had been transformed into a running track for the use of Logan Advertising.

At one end of the looping runway was the start line, and along the route large screens had been set up, which would be visible to the runners as they circuited.

"Everyone has their tags attached to their running shoes, and their recording devices?"

The little group responded with nods and upraised thumbs.

"The purpose of today is not to test the system, we know from the manufacturers it works properly," Matthew said. "What we need from you guys is feedback about the images you will see as you pass each screen. As you know, this technology has been used in marathons in the past few years, and don't worry, I'm not expecting anyone here to run a marathon unless they feel like one hell of a workout this morning." He grinned. "I'm going to do two circuits, because I need the exercise, but I think most people will do one. Susan has programmed the system with each runner's details. I'll let her explain the next bit."

Susan White stepped forward. "Okay, there are two parts to this, the runners…" The runners cheered. "And the supporters." The supporters cheered back. "Each runner has a team to keep them going. We're spreading the supporters out into four groups. Each group is covered by a camera. The RFID devices are triggered as each runner crosses over the mats set up along the route. This passes information on the runners' positions to central control. As each runner approaches the screen, a personalized message flicks up. They'll see real-time encouragement from their supporters, a targeted message from the advertisers, and as they pass, footage of the product."

"What we want to evaluate here today is the effectiveness of the advertising," Matthew said. "Each screen has the same information, but delivered in a different order. We've done some modeling in the office, but we need feedback from you guys as to which works best." He held up the recorder fastened on a lanyard around his neck. "As you see each screen, I want you to record the following information. Screen number, your thoughts about the content, and how you are feeling—both approaching the screen and leaving it." He pointed to the table set a little way away from the starting line. "When you've finished your run, hand in your recorder to Janice and she'll give you an envelope."

"No winners ribbons, boss?" one of the company's

directors, Jason shouted.

Matthew put his hands on his hips. "No, this isn't about who's the fastest, because that will be me, of course." Laughter rose in the air. "The envelopes are a thank you to everyone for volunteering. I'd love to take you all to the pub afterwards, but I know many of you have other things to do on a Saturday evening, so Janice has organized a little cash reward for helping out for you to spend as you wish. Taking your supporters out to dinner, maybe?"

He could tell this surprise was well received, and made a mental note to thank Janice later for thinking of the idea. When he'd put out the call for employees to give up their Saturday afternoon he'd been surprised by the instant positive response.

What had started as a test of the advertising campaign for their newest client had somehow morphed into a team-building exercise. The single members of the company seemed to be using it as a dating aid too. It hadn't escaped his notice that Jason had a team of three secretaries waving him on. Some of them had even made little flags.

There might well be some new couples by the time Monday morning swung around.

"Okay, are we ready?"

The runners took their position at the starting line, the supporters spread out behind the cameras, and the race began.

He'd only been half kidding about being the frontrunner. Although business had consumed most of his time this week, Matthew's usual routine of running three times a week meant he had a step up on most of his employees. As he approached the first screen, the rest of the field was far behind. The screen flashed up 'Matthew you're in the lead!' He grinned. Pressed the button to record. "First screen, feeling good about being in the lead." The image changed to a picture of Susan, who waved a flag with a self-conscious smile at the camera. "Feel good, having Susan waving," he recorded. Then as he drew level with the screen, a close up image of a runner's feet clad in Albios sneakers appeared with the company's logo above them. "The footage is too slow, I feel the urge to match my speed to theirs—it should be speeded up slightly. There could also be more information on this part; maybe we could insert the tagline. There's time for me to take in more information."

Satisfied, Matthew picked up the pace. Seeing a campaign in action was so much more effective than modeling it on the boardroom monitor. Heat spread through his thigh muscles as he pushed his body to its limit. The mix of runners, occasional joggers and walkers didn't matter. Each participant had at least one supporter, and as he passed the first group behind the camera, each person's enjoyment was evident.

Susan had volunteered to be his supporter, which was lucky, because he didn't have anyone to ask. Even though he got on well with everyone who worked for his company, the invisible boss-employee divide dictated none of them would be caught dead waving a flag and urging him on. For the first time in years, a trace of loneliness spread through him.

He dated, but kept his work and private life separate. And there was no one he could imagine wanting to see on the sidelines. Not that any of the women he dated would want to stand outside in the crisp spring air encouraging him on.

He approached the second screen, and dictated notes into his recording device. Everything about this campaign had to be perfect. Albios wanted to trial the campaign at a smaller 10k women-only race next month, and if all went well, Logan Advertising would be awarded the contract for advertising during the London Marathon.

This campaign was the big one. The one to cement their position as one of the most successful new advertising agencies in London. With the economy contracting, many of his rival firms had been forced to make redundancies; some had even gone out of business. The company he'd borrowed money from his parents and the bank to start five years ago bore his name. Everyone who worked within the spacious offices in one of London's steel and glass skyscrapers had mortgages to pay, families to support. There was no way Matthew would sacrifice any of them to the recession gods, not if he could help it.

His mother always called him stubborn.

Muscles burning, Matthew wiped the sweat from his brow as his feet pounded the asphalt.

Stubborn didn't begin to cover it.

Chapter Two

All work, no play, makes April a dull girl.

And I'm dull enough. April rubbed blusher onto her cheeks. If it had been up to her, she'd stay in again and watch another DVD. Her friends joked about the alphabetized stack on the shelf behind her TV, and sure, she had to admit she did have every rom-com ever produced, or at least every rom-com with her favorite leading men in them, but there wasn't anything wrong with that.

Marie and Eliza didn't agree. They were always telling her to stop watching life from the sidelines, and get out there and live it. She'd suggested a girls' night in, but this time they were adamant. The city had a lot to offer, and both of them were determined that tonight, they'd go out and sample a little bit of it.

As long as they didn't both hook up with gorgeous guys like last time. There was nothing fun about playing gooseberry.

She straightened the leather skirt Marie had persuaded her to buy in a moment of madness. How on earth was she going to sit down in this thing without flashing her panties to everyone? With a sigh, she turned away from the mirror.

She had time to make a phone call.

She sat on her bed and rested her hand on the phone.

Surely June had taken her advice, and given up the mad idea of inviting Matthew to the wedding? They hadn't had a chance to discuss it before June had headed back to Ireland.

She pulled in her bottom lip and chewed it. June wasn't an idiot. Even if Michael knew she'd been engaged once before, he couldn't possibly be okay with inviting her ex. And their parents would be livid. Mum's heart wasn't strong, she'd already had one heart attack, and the sight of Matthew Logan lounging in the pews would definitely add stress to what was already ramping up to be a stressful day.

Their father, Jack and his second wife Inez were flying in from Spain, and although both of her parents got on well enough most of the time, being seated next to each other on the top table would add more electricity into the mix. There was a real danger of electrocution, and if they clashed over Matthew...

It was tempting to just hope for the best, and ignore the situation. But in all honestly, she couldn't. Because Matthew's presence at the wedding held the potential to turn everyone's world upside down.

She dialed June's number.

June bubbled with wedding news. April dutifully reported on the dress's progress—at their final meeting she'd fitted June with the plain cotton toile mock-up of the dress, and made alterations. They'd finalized the final fabric, a heavy duchess satin in pale silver. June had brought Michael with her, so they hadn't had a chance to talk about the Matthew situation.

Bloody man. He's even become a situation.

June burbled on and on. April's eyes glazed over. She wasn't even remotely interested in the meal, the table settings, the flowers, but she obediently made the right noises for the following fifteen minutes. Then she snapped.

"June."

"And we thought for the buttonholes—"

"June." Raising her voice and lowering her tone had the desired effect.

"Hmm?"

"I want to talk to you about Matthew." April gritted her teeth.

"I've sent the invitations." Was there a trace of too-late in June's tone?

"You didn't invite him, did you? You know we agreed it wouldn't be a good…"

"You agreed inviting Matthew wouldn't be a good idea, I disagreed."

Oh crap, there definitely was more than a trace of too-late in June's voice, in fact it was more of a I've-done-it-get-over-it tone.

"June, you didn't."

"April, I did."

If she could see her sister now, April knew exactly what expression would be on June's face. She'd have her hands on her hips and her bottom jaw stuck out like a boxer inviting a punch. But she'd have her dukes up, ready to strike back.

"It'll cause no end of trouble."

"He's not a bad guy. Everyone blames him for—"

"Because he ran out on you, June. He's the goddamned runaway groom."

"He didn't leave me at the altar, April."

"Semantics." April squeezed her eyes tight shut. How

could June not realize that if Matthew attended the wedding he would be the sole topic of conversation?

If the press gets hold of it... She rubbed at the ache blooming in her forehead. Michael's family was practically American royalty. All of the newspapers would be there, and if one of them decided to do even basic research they'd discover June's history.

The past would only stay in the past as long as Matthew wasn't in the church.

The doorbell rang.

"Oh, who's that?" June jumped on the diversion like a cat pouncing on catnip.

"Marie and Eliza, we're..."

"You're going out? Great! Have a good night, we'll talk soon!"

A click. Dead air.

Was there actually such a place as Margeritaville? April licked the salt from the rim of her glass and followed it with a chilled mouthful of tequila. "We should have stuck to beer," she muttered. Her mouth tasted funny, as if her tongue had gone to sleep or something.

"Oh chill out. There's no work tomorrow." Marie pushed back her cloud of blonde hair, and adjusted her impressive cleavage. "This place is great, isn't it?"

April peered through the gloom. "It's sort of dark."

"Dark is good." Eliza helped herself to a handful of nuts from the little bowl on the table.

The house band switched to yet another soulful country tune.

"Why is it every country song in the universe is about broken hearts?"

"They're not all about broken hearts, they're all about love." Drink always brought out Marie's romantic side, and tonight was no different. "Love makes the world go round. Didn't you hear?"

"Love and broken hearts are the same thing." Her stupid sister had love. For the second time in her life. And she was willing to risk it, for what?

"You are in a crap mood this evening." Eliza cracked pistachios with her teeth, and added the shells to the mini pistachio mountain she'd got going on her side of the table. "If I didn't know better, I'd say you'd been a victim of a drive-by love shooting. What's going on?"

April never spoke about her sister's love life. There had been so much gossip about June's romance self-destructing; the family had put the whole subject on sacred-topic-never-to-be-discussed-outside-the-family alert.

Nope, she never talked about it. Except to Eliza and Marie.

"I called June before I came out."

There were twin moans from across the table.

"Your sister." Eliza grimaced.

"Your sister is a pain in the ass." Marie slammed her margarita onto the table. She waved her hands as though fighting off an influx of ninjas. "Okay, I know you don't want to hear a word about your sainted sister, but honestly, you take so much crap from her. She's always putting you down."

April's forehead hurt. She rubbed at the skin between her eyebrows. *What?*

"She does." Eliza's head jerked up and down in a nod so emphatic she looked like a bobble-headed doll. "You just don't see it. Every time you call her, or see her, you go all…

" She looked up, rubbed her jaw. "All sort of inferior."

"Inferior?" Her voice sounded ridiculously high. April swallowed. "What do you mean, inferior? I'm not inferior." Getting up and storming off wasn't really an option in these shoes, so April let her tone do the job for her.

Eliza rolled her eyes. Glanced at Marie.

"Look, what Eliza's trying to say is you talk about June as though she's a princess or something. As if she's better than you."

"She's had a hard time." They both knew June's history; it was inconceivable both her friends could be such bitches. Where was their empathy? Their female solidarity in the face of the awful thing that had happened to June?

"June had a relationship a long time ago that went wrong. She's never worked a day in her life, and now she's engaged to a man who will take care of her for the rest of her life. I honestly don't think she's had such a bad time." Eliza reached out and placed her hand over April's. "Your father's covered her rent for how long?"

"Well, she was upset, she needed—"

"She didn't need seven years to get over it." Eliza sipped her drink. "Look, I know you love her. But you're wearing rose-tinted glasses as far as your sister is concerned. She's had every advantage a girl could have, and she's happily taken every single one of them. Unlike you, she takes without giving back. She's not paying you for the dress, is she?"

"And you really can't afford to buy all the material, and the pearls and everything," Marie added. "I think she could have at least offered."

"I'm happy to make her dress. She's my sister." Okay, she could sort of see their point; it was no secret April's overdraft was stretched to the max to buy supplies for June's dress.

"Her fiancé is so rich he's hired a humongous yacht to sail her around the Caribbean for their honeymoon." Eliza's lip curled. "She buys everything from underwear to evening dresses in designer boutiques."

"She could have bought her dress from anywhere, but she chose me." April pried apart a pistachio nut and tossed the shell back into the bowl. "She chose me." June hadn't just picked her to make the dress because she was free. So why did doubt drip like chilled water down her spine?

"She chose you because you will make the perfect dress. You're a great designer," Marie said. "But she's taking advantage by not paying you for it."

"Hmm." April wanted to go home.

"I'm sorry. I didn't mean to wreck your buzz." Eliza's eyes glistened. "You know I think you're fantastic, don't you? It's just your sister really annoys me. And you brought her up. What happened on the phone call?"

April shot her a side-eyes glance.

Eliza pressed a finger to her lips. "I promise not to bash June any more. No matter what."

Her friend looked so sincere, April relented. "She's sent out the invitations. And she invited Matthew."

Marie gasped. "Matthew? The runaway—"

"Surely you told her..." Eliza said.

"Yes, I told her it was a completely stupid move, but she did it anyway."

Eliza squeezed her lips together. Put both hands over her mouth, like the speak-no-evil monkey. She shook her head.

With Eliza on shut-down, Marie's voice broke the

silence.

"So what are you going to do about it?"

*****

Matthew recognized the handwriting on the thick ivory envelope immediately, even though he hadn't seen it for years—since he'd been a kid passing notes in class. June's handwriting wasn't even particularly distinctive, there was no reason why it should be so instantly recognizable, but memory was pervasive.

He tapped the heavy envelope, half hoping to discern its purpose without having to actually open it. He hated revisiting the past, filled as it was with long discarded pain and anger. Over the past seven years, he'd changed so much his past self was a stranger to the man he was today.

He placed the envelope carefully on the rosewood table inside the front door, and stalked away as though escaping an unexploded bomb.

The house was too empty without Ben. His dog had lived for many more years than anyone expected, but eventually old age and disease had caught up with him. Matthew's mother had been trying to persuade him to move on, to share his home and time with a puppy, but the time wasn't right. He was so busy with work he didn't have the right to bring a new dog into his life. Besides he was rarely here, spending most of his time at the office. When Ben was alive, he'd worked in his home office at weekends, but now...

Now, there was nothing keeping him at home. Nothing that needed him.

He levered open a window and breathed in the cool evening air. Why would June contact him after all these years?

With a curse, he stalked back to the table and snatched up the envelope.

The card inside was a wedding invitation, wrapped in a folded piece of paper.

We were friends once, her familiar looped handwriting wrote. *I'm getting married, and I'd love you to come.* The note was signed with love, then her signature. Matthew read the details of the wedding. He didn't recognize the name of her intended, but she'd chosen to wed in the church they'd decided on so many years ago. As it was the only church in Brookbridge, the village they'd both grown up in, that was no surprise.

If any of his family knew June Leigh was getting married they would have told him, so he guessed he was the only member of his family to receive an invitation. All ties with the Leighs had been cut after the wedding was called off. He'd told Amy she should stay friends with April, the two of them had always been closer than sisters, but she'd been adamant at breaking off relations.

Matthew had moved on in more ways than one. Luckily he'd done well enough in his end-of-year exams to have a choice of places to complete his third level education, and had chosen the option as far as possible from Brookbridge. His family had mourned his move to the UK as though he'd emigrated to Australia.

Every time he returned home, the prospect of running into June or her mother on the street cast a cloud over everything. People in the town, people he'd known his whole life, still looked away when he walked into the local shops. The town had a long memory.

Inviting him to her wedding…

He ran his thumb over her words. Maybe in some

twisted way she thought inviting him to the wedding would heal the wounds, would show everyone she'd made peace with the past. Rehabilitation—June style.

Matthew ripped the invitation in two, and dropped it into the wastebasket.

*****

Dad usually rang on Sundays, and today was no exception.

"Inez wants some insider info on what color dress she should wear for the wedding." He sounded tired. "I don't see that it matters, but she says it really does. So I'm asking."

"I don't know about Michael's mother, but Mum is wearing light blue, and I'm wearing a sort of dusky rose."

"That's pink, right?"

"Tell her dusky rose, she'll get it."

"Light blue and dusky rose, Inez," Jack called.

April smiled as she heard her stepmother in the background.

Jack sighed. "Now she wants to know about hats."

A call from Inez.

"Okay, okay, fascinators. What the hell is a fascinator anyway?"

"It's a sort of headdress, Dad. Tell her Mum is wearing a hat, and I've got pearls in my hair."

"Jeez, it's so complicated." Her father was quickly losing patience with all things feminine. "The wedding is a month away. I don't see why everyone is getting so het up."

April scooted up in bed, rearranged the pillows, and pulled her duvet close. "It matters, Dad. We just want everything to be perfect." She plucked at the duvet cover, and wished she'd managed to get a glass of water before her father's call. Her head was pounding as though an army of jackhammer-wielding builders were having a party.

She closed her eyes. She rarely drank, and this morning she remembered why.

Hangovers suck.

Her father droned on. "Come on, what could go wrong?"

She almost told him.

"June said Michael's family have block-booked the hotel, apparently they have security travelling with them. His father sounds a real hotshot. I'm booking a room today for Inez and me. Do you want me to book one for you too?"

"I'm going to stay with Mum." Her mother had announced she wanted to sleep in her own house after the wedding, and April had voted to join her. It was bound to be an emotional day, and at least this way they could spend some quality time together.

"Okay. June seems happy?"

"Yes, I think so." It was natural her father would be worried about his eldest daughter. After all, he'd been here before and seen it all gone wrong.

"She deserves some happiness. I haven't seen that young buck since he ran. Even after all these years..." He made a familiar sound, the sound he made when sucking through his teeth.

"It's a long time ago." April tried to infuse her tone with soothing.

"Not long enough. I swear if I see him again I'll deck him."

The pain in her jaw alerted her to the fact she was grinding her teeth again. She slackened her jaw, opened and mouth and breathed in and out.

So June hadn't told him then. *Fan-bloody-tastic.* A part

..r, the part that had nursed a crush on Matthew all those years ago almost felt sorry for him. No doubt, he'd come to the wedding under the impression he was being welcomed back into the fold, when in fact there were a whole pack of wolves ready and waiting to tear him limb from limb.

If June hadn't told Dad, she wouldn't have told Mum either, which meant the best possible scenario was Mum would dissolve into tears as her ex ranted and raved, or have a heart attack with the stress.

There was nothing for it—someone needed to save the situation, and despite the lack of a superhero costume, it would have to be April to the rescue.

Chapter Three

It was more channeling James Bond than Superwoman. Sure, she wasn't a six foot hunk, but April was pretty pleased with her investigative skills. It was pretty easy, actually. A search of the London phone book had only returned one Matthew Logan, and she'd carefully copied down his address.

Now, like Monsieur Bond, she would painstakingly track her quarry and use her seduction skills to charm him into not attending the wedding. How hard could it be?

Start with sugar, and if necessary, she had arm flailing freaking out to fall back on. One of her approaches would definitely work. Because failure wasn't an option.

She looked crap in a tux, so instead, she'd strapped on high heels that made the best of her legs, and dressed in a leather mini and a black shirt—because it was winter, and black was her winter color. Now she stood at his front door.

April plastered on a bright smile and pressed the bell.

He wouldn't remember her. It had been years...

The door opened.

Her mouth went slack.

The Matthew in front of her was even more good-looking than he'd been back then. In a fraction of a second her gaze drank him in. The years had added a few lines to the corners of his cobalt eyes. His mouth was just as she remembered, firm and sexy. His dark chocolate hair stood up in front, as though he'd run his fingers through it seconds before opening the door. Her gaze dropped. Those shoulders... Years ago, he'd been lanky. Now? He looked as though he'd worked out every day of the last seven years.

He wore shorts and sneakers, with strong corded thighs covered in a dusting of dark hair on full display. April swallowed.

How was she to remain detached faced with such male beauty?

"Can I help you?" His voice was deep. His gaze did the whole up-down-full-body-scan thing she'd just done to him, lingering for a moment on her legs, as though even if he didn't recognize her face, he might recognize her legs.

"Matthew." Darn it, her voice was so high, she sounded like a cheerleader.

"Yes." His eyes narrowed.

"You probably don't remember me, it's been a long time..."

His eyes widened. "April?"

She nodded. "April. I'm sorry for turning up unannounced, but I...I want to talk to you."

"April Leigh." His mouth curved into a smile.

Her stomach flipped. Somehow she'd forgotten that smile.

"God, it's been years." He stepped back, and held the door open wide. "Come on in."

"Were you going out?"

"I was just going for a jog. It can wait." He closed the

door.

Large London houses like these were often divided into flats, but this one had only one doorbell, and there was no evidence Matthew's house was subdivided. A Persian rug lay atop the polished wooden floorboards. The walls were painted warm terracotta and cluttered with what looked like nineteenth-century prints.

"Come on into the kitchen."

She followed him down the long hallway into the room at the end. His back view was just as attractive as the front. She snapped her gaze from his butt to the back of his head. This wasn't a guy she could lust over. This was Matthew. Runaway Groom. More hemlock than catnip. *Focus.*

He flicked on the kettle, and waved her to a chair around the worn wooden kitchen table. The way he looked at her, as if he'd never seen her before, did something funny to her stomach.

"You've really changed." His head tilted to the side. "I almost didn't recognize you."

"But you did."

He smiled. "It's your eyes. Eyes never change, do they?"

He remembered her eyes? April blinked.

"What's your poison. Tea? Coffee?"

"Coffee. Black, please."

He spooned granules into a cup and brought two cups to the table. He turned a chair around and sat, resting his elbows on its back. His sexual lure was so strong her mouth dried.

"So, what brings you to London, April?"

"I live here." Sitting here with him was so strange. Once they'd been as easy around each other as family. Now, the air seemed to buzz with things unsaid. The last time she'd seen him she'd been in school. Once been almost family; now they knew nothing about each other.

She took a sip of coffee and burned the top of her mouth. "After I finished school I came to London to study fashion. I qualified, and now I'm putting together my first collection."

"Clothes?" His gaze dipped to her feet. "Or shoes maybe? That pair is wicked."

She flexed her toes. "Have you a thing for shoes?" The moment the words left her mouth she wished she could call them back. Especially when he arched a black brow.

"I can appreciate a woman's shoes as much as the next man."

Heat flared into April's face.

"But more for what they do to a woman's legs than anything else. Obviously."

He was looking at her ankles.

She crossed them. Bond had never found himself in this situation. She felt as gauche and flustered as she had when she was a teenager. But she wasn't a teenager anymore. She was a woman. With a mission.

April gritted her teeth. Took a long look from his powerful calves to his big feet. "I like your shoes too." Her voice sounded husky. Flirty husky.

His gaze shot up. The eyes that met hers held an expression of stunned disbelief. As though he'd been playing with a puppy that had suddenly bared its teeth and then torn a chunk out of his hand.

Once upon a time, he'd have joked it away.

He stretched his foot out. Twisted his ankle back and forth. "They're Albios."

Designer sneakers? Obviously Matthew had moved up

in the world. Big house, fancy shoes. What else?

"You know Albios, right?"

"Are you a shoe snob? Because I can't afford Manolos."

He glanced at her shoes again. "Those do the job."

Whatever job that was remained unspecified.

"So." He rubbed the trace of dark stubble on his chin with his knuckles. "Why are you here?"

*****

April Leigh looked nothing like her sister. June had modeled herself after an old-time screen goddess, like Marilyn or Zaza,Zsa Zsa all blonde and curvy. Even as a teen she dressed to make the most of her assets, and was always perfectly made up.

April, on the other hand, was as natural as they come. She might be wearing make-up, for surely no woman had eyelashes as long and dark as hers naturally, but her skin was pale with a dusting of faint freckles. Her hair, sparrow brown, was straight and long, pulled back from her face with a tortoiseshell clasp. Her full mouth was unadorned by lipstick. The moment Matthew wondered what it might feel like against his, he looked away.

At first, he'd been thrown off by her long legs and unfamiliar curves. But then he'd recognized her eyes. Cornflower blue with little gold specks. They at least were familiar.

She'd been shy, back then. Sort of uncoordinated, always bumping into things. But she'd been cute and fun. He remembered the conversations they had while he was waiting for June to be ready to go out. Talks about the universe, about her desire to become a vet. Where had that girl gone?

The April who sat at his kitchen table was all grown up.

She eyed him with suspicion through guarded eyes. The exchange of words about his legs and hers had definitely held a trace of flirt. And to be honest, if they'd met for the first time today, he'd have no compunction about acting on the attraction which had flared pretty darned instantly the moment he'd seen her standing on his doorstep. Flirting was as natural as breathing, with the right person.

She wasn't the right person.

Matthew crossed his arms.

She'd started to fidget the moment he asked the question. Her throat moved. She seemed to be summoning all her resources, as if preparing for battle.

The air was thick with anticipation. If she were a friend, he'd take pity on her and change the subject, but he wanted her answer so he let it be.

She twisted a lock of hair between her fingers. Bit her bottom lip. Then blasted him with her cornflower gaze. "I've come to talk to you about June's wedding."

An unfamiliar anger exploded through Matthew like an electric shock.

Typical. June was all about making those who loved her do her bidding. His non-response to the invitation must have irritated her, and so she'd sent April to get an acceptance.

There was no way he was playing this game.

"You must have better things to do than visit all of her guests to make sure they've received their invitations." He rubbed the back of his head. "You can tick me off, I got one."

Let June stew. There was absolutely no way in hell he'd go to her wedding. Not stating his intentions was petty, but petty felt good. In fact, the prospect of leaving June in the lurch, wondering if he was going to turn up, was incredibly satisfying.

"Are you going?" April tilted her jaw up a fraction.

The smooth curve of her neck was lean and smooth. He wanted to trace it with his fingers. Matthew gritted his teeth. "I think that's between June and me, don't you?" This conversation was over. Matthew stood. "It's been good to see you, April, but I really should get a run in." He walked around the table to her, in an unmistakable get-out-of-here move.

She didn't get up. "June doesn't know I'm here." She swallowed. "Please give me a moment of your time."

He looked closer.

Her throat moved and she seemed to have paled to milk-white.

"She didn't send you?"

"No." Her hands clenched into fists on the lap of her short leather skirt. "June told me she invited you, and I came to ask you not to come."

The thought of attending June's wedding hadn't been remotely appealing, but this—April's insistence that he shouldn't—sparked his interest. "Why not?"

"Would you sit?"

He was still looming over her, and it seemed, making her nervous.

He pulled out the chair nearest to her and sat.

"The thing is… Well…the past is over. She's moved on, and you must have moved on too."

He nodded.

"I mean, going to the wedding might make your girlfriend insecure, and…"

"What if there's no girlfriend?"

"There's no girlfriend?" Her eyes widened a fraction. She chewed on her bottom lip.

"Not at the moment, no."

"Ah." Her eyes darted to the kitchen table, as though the pot of marmalade dead center was incredibly interesting. "I don't know why June invited you, but surely you can see that going to the wedding would be foolish."

"Foolish?" Matthew frowned. Did she think he was going to run off with her sister or something?

"Foolish. Because I don't think she's told her fiancé she invited you. And his parents are very conservative. I don't think they'd approve."

"She has told her fiancé about her past, I presume?"

"Yes, but knowing about you and having you at their wedding are very different things." She smoothed her hair back. "Michael could be confused, could be hurt…"

"Have you a crush on your sister's fiancé, April?" he asked quietly.

She frowned. "Of course not. He's not my type."

Immediately Matthew found himself wondering what exactly was her type. Was he her type? He rubbed his neck and wished this whole situation wasn't happening. It would be easy to stop it; all he had to do was tell her he had no intention of attending the wedding. But she hadn't come out with the true reason she was so frantic he shouldn't go. And letting her off the hook at this point would mean he'd never know.

"My mother has a weak heart, and my father…"

June's father had always been a bulldog. "Your father what?"

"My father isn't in the mood for keeping the past in the past. If you come to the wedding I'm sure he'll make a scene."

So even so many years later, June hadn't come clean about what had happened between them. If he'd cared about June, he would have been disappointed. Now, paradoxically, the only thing that rankled was the knowledge that April considered him a total bastard.

"Why should he make a scene?" He knew the answer, but couldn't resist goading her into saying it.

"You're the runaway groom. You left my sister when she needed you." Her lip curled in obvious distain. "You've broken her heart once, are you really ready to ruin her future?"

Anger blazed through Matthew in a heated rush. He clenched his teeth and breathed in through his nose. The urge to throw her out, to tell her straight up to just go to hell was a strong one.

His hands shook. "I can be civilized. I'm sure your parents can be to. And June wants me there."

She closed her eyes for a brief moment, then opened them again. "I'm begging you not to go. I'll do anything."

"Anything?"

Her mouth opened into a perfect O at his whispered word.

"I'm irritated you consider me some sort of monster, April." He reached out and stroked her bare arm. "I think you don't really know me at all."

Her gaze met his, and for the life of him he couldn't look away.

"I think you need to get to know me better. I haven't replied to the invitation yet, and maybe I'll go, maybe not. I'm certainly not going to decline just because you think badly of me."

"I…"

"If you want me not to go to the wedding, you'll have to persuade me of the folly of going. And you're going to have to shelve the contempt you feel."

Her gaze flickered to his mouth.

"We can start tomorrow night, over dinner." He stood. "Write down your phone number."

Chapter Four

As an emergency talkathon was needed, Marie and Eliza came over for Sunday lunch. April had cooked a stuffed chicken with rosemary and roast potatoes, and had made cauliflower cheese, and gravy. Comfort food.

The table was set. Marie poured three glasses of chardonnay, and they sat down at the table. "So, what's going on?"

April hadn't wanted to go into it on the phone, so her friends were clueless about the situation she'd gotten herself into.

"I am going out to dinner tomorrow night."

"With a man? Woo! Go you!" Eliza's cheerleading made everything worse.

April groaned and rubbed her forehead.

"Ah, not woo?" Eliza asked.

"Definitely not woo." April swallowed a mouthful of wine. "I think I've really screwed up."

"What's going on?" Marie took a mouthful of food, and raised her eyes heavenward. "This is delicious."

"I went to see Matthew, to ask him not to go to the wedding."

Marie's eye's opened so wide she looked as though she'd been electrocuted. "You...what?"

"What's he like?" Eliza asked.

"He was always good-looking, but now...well let's just say he's improved with age." With Eliza and Marie she could be totally honest, and the turmoil swirling around in her gut since yesterday needed an outlet. "He's irresistibly gorgeous. I flirted with him."

Marie did goldfish face. Her mouth opened and closed, but no words came out.

"I didn't mean to." April pulled her black tee-shirt out of her jeans. Her stomach felt hot. "I wore the black skirt and the way he looked at my legs...well I just couldn't help it." She took another mouthful of wine.

"He flirted back, I take it?"

Self-disgust flooded April. "Yes, he flirted back. I feel dirty. I liked it." What sort of a woman flirted with the man who'd made her sister pregnant and then ran out on her? "I'm a total monster."

"The whole thing with your sister is over and done." Marie tossed her hair back. "You once said you had a crush on him years ago."

"Every girl with a pulse had a crush on Matthew Logan. But there's no way I can get involved with him. It would be the ultimate betrayal of June. The guy is a snake."

"So why are you going out with him? Eliza asked.

"I asked him not to go to the wedding." She remembered the hint of hurt in his eyes that had appeared for a brief moment. "I sort of gave him hell for running out on her years ago."

"Ouch," Marie said.

"Yeah, ouch. I think I made him really angry. He told

me I'd formed a wrong impression of him. That I need to get to know him better. Tomorrow night is to be the first step."

Maria pushed a roast potato around, covering it with gravy. "He might have a point; after all there are two sides to every story. You might even get to like the guy."

Liking Matthew wasn't an option. "Hmm."

"Keep an open mind. Go to dinner. Treat him like a human being, rather than the pariah he actually is. You can ease into it; make him see how going to the wedding would be a bad idea. What could possibly go wrong?" Eliza was a perennial optimist.

Maria nodded. "I agree, you just need to charm him a little. Then you can talk to him as a friend. Appeal to his better side."

April forced a smile. There was no way it would be that easy. But what choice did she have?

*****

He had no idea why he'd asked her out. The more he'd thought about it in the day since, the more he'd been convinced he must be having some sort of a breakdown. Maybe he was going totally crazy. Because getting to know April Leigh better was a recipe for disaster.

It had been a long time since the opinion of others made even a dent in his outer shell. But the look on her face as she damned him for treating June badly had hurt. April had been a friend. His little sister Amy's best friend. Condemnation from her somehow was worse than the cold shoulder he got from certain people in Brookbridge. It was personal. There was no way he'd tell her the truth about her sister, but at the same time he wasn't going to suffer her disdain.

He would ignore the fact that she was hot.

Not flirting would be difficult, but tonight he'd have to try. He loved women, and in the past few years had spent time with quite a few of them. But he'd unerringly pulled back at the first hint a relationship was turning more serious. Once he'd thought he understood someone, had trusted completely. And look where that had got him.

There were thousands of restaurants he could take her to. Hundreds of clubs, and countless places to go. This evening was about getting to know each other, about cutting the thread with the past, and connecting as adults. They'd need distraction, something different to achieve that, so he'd suggested meeting at the Embankment Underground station.

He pushed back the sleeve of his white shirt and glanced at his watch.

When he looked up, she was walking toward him. Her hair was twisted up in a complicated knot, and she was wearing a long black coat and high black boots.

"Hi." Her voice was slightly breathless.

He stepped forward and kissed her cheek, breathing in her warm, spicy perfume. Kissing a friend was natural, automatic, innocuous. But as he eased away, her rapid breathing was impossible to ignore. Her lips parted a fraction, and her gaze flickered to his mouth.

"We're walking." He slipped an arm through hers and walked her across the road, to Embankment Pier.

As they approached, April's fingers clasped tighter. "Oh, are we going here?" Delight shone from the face she tilted his direction. "I've always wanted to go on one of these!"

"Me too." Matthew smiled. "In all the years I've lived here, I've never done the tourist thing, but I thought seeing as both of us are essentially foreigners in a strange land, we'd both enjoy it."

"Great choice."

The custom-made boat was like a floating dining room, with polished wooden floors and the entire top and sides made of glass. Candles flickered on each table. The hostess led them to a secluded table at the side of the floor, which gave a perfect view of London. She whisked away April's coat.

Beneath it, she wore a long black dress, clinched in at the waist with a studded leather belt. It dipped low in the front, revealing a glimpse of creamy cleavage. The only flash of color came from the red gemstones encased in gold around her throat.

"You look beautiful. Is that one of your creations?"

April blushed. "Yes."

Matthew raised one of the glasses of Kir the waitress brought to the table. "Here's to getting to know each other better."

"I'll drink to that." She brought the glass to her lips and sipped. She gazed out through the expanse of window. "The view is fantastic."

"We'll get going in a moment, apparently we'll see all of London." He pulled a brochure from his pocket and read it aloud. "London Bridge, the Houses of Parliament, Tower Bridge, The Millennium Dome…"

"Wow." Her delighted grin was unforced.

"A jazz band will be playing later too."

"I could get addicted to this."

"I'm glad you approve." He picked up a menu. "So now we know one thing for sure about each other. We both enjoy surprises."

"Well…" She tilted her head to the side. "Some surprises aren't good."

He shook his head. "We are not talking about the wedding."

She frowned.

"Talking about the wedding is a bad idea. How can we relax while we're both trying to influence each other? We'll talk about it a month from today."

"A month?"

"Not a single word about the wedding for a month. That's my final offer."

"I know something else about you." A hint of a smile tilted the corners of her mouth up. "You're stubborn."

"You better believe it." He handed her a menu. "Let's choose, I'm starving."

This idea for dinner had really been a masterstroke. The constantly changing view beyond the glass walls was a useful point of conversation, smoothing over any awkward lulls. Matthew talked about his job, and by the time dessert was served, April was considerably more relaxed.

"Our client, Albios, are sponsoring a 10k race before the London Marathon which we hope will prove as a testing ground for all of the elements of our advertising campaign," he explained. "The face is female only, so we've been doing extensive testing with female runners."

"What's the difference?"

"Mainly in the approach. Our market research showed our female staff wanted to see their families and supporters for longer, and straight away, with the advertising punch coming at the end of the segment, when they were running away from the sign rather than before."

"Makes sense. I'd be anticipating seeing my friends

shouting me on as I ran up to the sign."

"We also discovered if we stretched the advertising at the end of the segment for another couple of minutes, it acted as a lead in to the next runner."

"So the screen was more or less permanently displaying something?"

Matthew nodded. He raised an eyebrow, tapped the wine bottle, then when she agreed, refilled her glass. "A lot of these details can only be worked out in a live environment—which is why we're running another trial in a couple of weeks."

He smiled. "I doubt I'll be able to persuade my employees to sacrifice more of their spare time to test it out though. It might just end up being the directors."

"I'll come and try it out if you like." She really didn't *do* jogging, but how hard could it be to run along with a group of office workers in the countryside?

Life had been lived inside for months, either working on her collection or in the coffee-shop. Now she was on top of her workload, the thought of taking some time out and giving her body a workout at the same time was appealing.

"That would be great. Would you come as my supporter or as a runner?"

"As a runner." No doubt Matthew would be too busy breaking the speed record to notice if she jogged a while, walked a bit. And afterwards she could crawl home and collapse, if need be.

"If Amy lived closer I'd hound her into it too."

Warmth spread through April's chest. Memories of endless days and evenings spent laughing with her friend sparkled like crystals in the dark cave of her mind. For once, she didn't try to force them away with remembered quarrels they'd had about the wedding that never happened. In this moment she just recalled the fun. The love. The good times.

"Where is she now?" Her voice sounded wistful, but Matthew didn't seem to notice.

"New York."

She knew nothing at all about one of her oldest friends. "What's she doing?"

"She's still organizing those trips…" His gaze sharpened. "You don't know, do you? About…"

"I don't know anything about her anymore." April pushed her plate away. "We lost touch a long time ago."

The room filled with the sound of softly played jazz, and a few couples stepped onto the dance floor, drifting around with glittering London as a backdrop.

"Would you like to dance?"

Yes, she'd like to dance. She'd like to soothe the melancholy that somehow had lodged in her heart, as though she'd breathed it in, like mist.

Dancing with Matthew was beyond foolish.

She reached for the tiny white porcelain cup of espresso. "I think I better drink my coffee." A glance at her watch revealed they'd been on the ship for hours. The night was almost over.

There was no way to cut the evening short, no way to call a taxi and escape into the night. Not yet, anyway.

"Amy works for a company in New York organizing camera safaris in Africa for rich Americans. She says she does it because as a side benefit, she gets to act as liaison once a year, and go with them."

With the conversation back on a neutral footing, April breathed in deep and imagined Amy creeping up on antelope.

"She was always crazy for adventures."

"She hadn't changed a bit. Last year, she managed to talk her way onto an expedition to Peru." Matthew leaned close. "She came back dressed like an Inca—she sent me a picture and I swear everything she was wearing was either red or embroidered."

Amy had always been a flamboyant adventure seeker.

"Hang on, I might have it." Matthew pulled out his wallet and tugged a photograph from the back panel. "Yup, thought so." He handed it over.

Amy's long hennaed hair curled around her face. A richly embroidered hat sat atop the curls. She was grinning in the picture, and every inch of her was covered by bright Inca clothing. She wore strings of beads around her neck. "She looks great."

"You wanted to be a vet. How the heck did you end up designing dresses?"

April thought back through the years to the girl she'd been. A year after Matthew had run out on the wedding, her parents' marriage had come unstuck. Dad had a job opportunity in Spain and he'd taken it. Mum had been so demoralized she'd spent the next six months moping around the house.

April's focus had shifted. They were the same—she and Mum. Both slender and athletic, sort of shy, and guarded. June dressed every day in knockout clothes, and attacked the world, and it had occurred to April if her mother could borrow some of that chutzpah it would give her the confidence to go on.

"Mum needed a job, and when an opportunity came along, her confidence was at rock-bottom." They'd rooted through her mother's wardrobe, looking for the perfect outfit. "She didn't have anything to wear. Well, not anything that played to her strengths and gave her confidence. I took her shopping, and when I got her to try on this one dress… " April's mouth curved. The designer dress didn't look much on the hanger, but it transformed Margaret. The cleverly-cut navy shift had a V neckline ideal to show-off Margaret's long neck. It clung in all the right places, giving the illusion of curves. Finally, the half-sleeves that came to her elbow covered the area she was most insecure about.

"Mum looked great. And her confidence was so high, she rocked the interview and got the job." Some women like June and Amy, were so full of confidence they could wear anything. Others felt so awkward in clothes, dressing was a nightmare. Clothes were too tight, too low cut, too badly fitting. It didn't have to be like that, not if the designer's emphasis was on the wearer, rather than transitory fashion trends. Becoming a designer was more than April's job, it was her calling. She wanted the look of delight that had been on her mother's face back then to be on the faces of all the women who wore her clothes.

She wanted to give them armor. "I want to make dresses that make women feel good."

Matthew smiled. "Dress for success, huh?" He nodded. "I can see how that works. Men don't usually have as many clothes as women, my wardrobe is stuffed full of Amy's things for when she's visiting. I have six suits." A dimple flashed in his cheek. "But I bet they cost more than all her clothes put together."

"And you feel great when you wear them?"

"Always." He glanced out of the window. "We're docking."

Despite her misgivings, the evening had been a pleasant

one.

"I enjoyed…" April's cell phone rang. "Oh, excuse me for a moment." She answered it.

"April, it's Elizabeth." Her boss's tone was urgent. "Where are you?"

"I'm out having dinner. What's up?"

As Elizabeth spoke, dread floated like a black fog at the top of April's head, then gradually sank downward, chilling every inch of her insides.

She hung up. "There's been a fire." April reached down for her bag. "I have to go." She rolled her lips together as her gaze flickered to the exit.

Matthew laid a hand on her sleeve. "Where? Tell me what happened."

She ran a hand over her face. "There was a fire at the coffee shop I work in. The one directly under my apartment. That was my boss and landlady, Elizabeth. She says the coffee shop is a write-off. I don't know what state my apartment is in." She paled. Her hands clutched into fists. "All of my collection is in the apartment. There's bound to be smoke damage…"

"There's no point in panicking until we get there." He stood and asked the waitress for April's coat.

She flashed him a wobbly goodbye smile. "Thanks for tonight, I had fun."

"You're not going by yourself." He took her elbow. "I parked nearby, I'll drive you."

"You don't need…" She shook her head, doubtless considering how long it would take her to get home on the tube. "Actually I'd appreciate a lift."

"Of course." April was alone in London, facing a possible disaster, there was no way he'd let anyone endure that alone.

She was quiet as his powerful car cut through London's streets, except for giving directions occasionally in clipped tones.

"Do you have somewhere to stay tonight?"

She darted him a glance. "I'm sure it won't come to that. If so, I have a couple of friends I could call."

Matthew looked at the clock on the dash. "You can stay with me. It's too late to arrive at a friend's house."

She pointed.

A fire engine was parked outside the coffee shop, and a small crowd were gathered on the sidewalk. It looked worse than they'd imagined.

"There's Elizabeth."

He pulled up and let her out, searching the road for a parking space. By the time he made it back to her, she was deep in conversation with a woman wearing sweats.

Quickly she made the introductions.

"I need to get upstairs."

Elizabeth nodded. "I used my key to let the firefighters in. The flames didn't reach the apartment, but you can't stay there tonight. The air is toxic."

His mother would have been wailing to heaven in this situation, but April stayed calm and focused in the face of this bad news.

Her gaze met his, then she stepped away from the crowd, to the narrow doorway on the right of the coffee shop.

He followed.

The acrid smell of smoke hung in the air. The door to her apartment was open, and inside a man who could only be the fire chief was assessing the situation.

"This is my tenant." A voice from behind them. He hadn't noticed Elizabeth following.

April walked to a rack of clothes. She ran her hands over them, as if checking they were still intact. She lifted a dress to her face, then pushed it away with a grimace.

"Sorry, love. But everything here is smoke-damaged." The fire chief's face was covered in black smears. "I'm afraid you won't be able to stay here."

"For how long?" Her voice was no louder than a whisper.

He shook his head. Whistled in air through his teeth. "Obviously you'll need access to remove your possessions. But it'll be weeks."

April looked at the ground and rubbed her face. "If the fire didn't penetrate the apartment..."

Elizabeth spoke. "Downstairs is gutted, April. The whole building's structure may well be unsafe." Her eyes filled with tears. "The insurance will cover everything in the apartment of course, but rebuilding—" She broke off in a sob.

To Matthew's amazement, April walked over to the older woman and put her arm around her shoulders. "Do you have anyone here for you?" Her voice was filled with concern.

In the midst of her own tragedy, rather than blaming the other woman or indulging in a totally justified pity-party, she was concerned for someone else. He shouldn't really be surprised, April had always been selfless.

"My husband is outside." Elizabeth wiped her eyes on the sleeve of her sweatshirt. "I'm so sorry, April. All your stuff..." She looked at the table stacked with threads and material. The rack of clothing. "Your collection..."

April pulled in a deep breath. Her spine straightened, as though someone had pulled her shoulders back. "There's not much I can do tonight." She turned to the fire chief. "Can I get back in here tomorrow to organize removing my things?"

"I'll be here at nine," he said.

Matthew rested his hand on her shoulder. "Pack a bag."

There was no protesting, no more talk of going to find a friend to stay with for tonight. Her head jerked, then she walked into the bedroom.

Matthew pulled a couple of business cards from his pocket, and jotted numbers on the back of both. He handed one to Elizabeth and one to the chief. "April will be staying with me. These are my numbers."

Chapter Five

Matthew didn't speak as he drove the powerful car through the rain-dashed streets.

April wrapped her arms around the rucksack of clothes and essentials she'd hastily packed. A faint scent of smoke clung to everything. She tugged the drawstring open. Pulled an inch of her tee-shirt from the bag and smelled it. The smell of smoke was so much stronger, they'd be no way she could wear any of this stuff without washing it.

"Have you a washing machine?"

Matthew's gaze didn't waver from the road. His tanned hands were relaxed on the wheel. Through the whole ordeal he'd been steady and calm, a rock in a rapidly shifting sea of shocks.

"Yes, and a dryer. I'll put them in when we get home, so you can have something clean and fresh to wear tomorrow."

"You're very kind to—"

"Forget it." His jaw tightened. "Anyone would do the same."

Not everyone. Once, sitting in a coffee shop, April had spotted a woman who'd made her life hell in school. They hadn't seen each other for years, and doubtless the adult was very different to the bratty kid she'd once been. She was dressed in skyscraper heels, and clutching a tray laden with salad and latte. With every teetering step she risked tripping. And with her hands unable to save herself, she'd face-plant for sure.

April thought about how she would react should her idle daydream become reality. If a stranger fell, she'd instantly dash from her seat and help her up. Sympathy would well up from nowhere as she identified with a stranger's plight. It had happened before.

But with someone she knew—someone who's cruel nature and mean jibes had hurt her? She'd leave her lying.

Despite the fact her family had no time for Matthew, that she had shunned his sister, unwilling to even talk about the end of their siblings relationship, Matthew had proffered a hand of friendship which she really didn't deserve.

At his house, Matthew showed her to the spare room. He opened the wardrobe and rooted around for a moment, then placed two items of clothing on the bed. "These are Amy's. Why don't you get dressed? I'll make some cocoa and put your clothes in the machine."

With a grimace at the stench of smoke, April separated her clothing from her other possessions and handed them over.

"I'll see you downstairs." Arms laden, Matthew retreated.

I'm so damned tired.

April stripped off her dress and underwear and dressed in the worn cotton onesie.

The grey sweatshirt must have been one of Matthews,

it reached her knees, but she didn't care about her appearance. Not while everything that constituted her world was lost.

She found a pair of Amy's fur-lined slippers in the wardrobe, slipped them on, and went downstairs.

Matthew stood in front of a blazing fire. Even though they were gas generated, the flickering flames were mesmerizingly real.

He pointed to the table in front of the fire. "Cocoa's here." He'd even put out a few oversize chocolate chip cookies on a blue plate.

"Nice onesie." He smiled. "Ducks look good on you."

Never in her wildest dreams would she have bought nightclothes with yellow plastic ducks printed on them.

"It's comfortable." She sank onto the sofa and reached for the mug, curling her fingers around its welcome warmth. She should thank him, tell him she'd be out of his hair soon, but right now all she wanted to do was close her eyes and wish this whole stinking situation away. There were so many things to do. She'd have to talk to the insurance people, find somewhere else to live, find another job...

The list was overwhelming. Endless. She'd said she could stay with a friend, but both of her close friends lived in one-bedroom flats. There wouldn't be room for any of her stuff, and even though they'd happily take her in, it would be a terrible imposition. If she had any relatives in England she could prevail on them, but all her family lived across the sea.

"You're frowning." Matthew sat next to her.

"I'm just trying to…" It was too difficult to put into words. There were too many things to think about.

"Drink your cocoa before it goes cold." Matthew drank

his, leaving a milky chocolate trail across his top lip.

She couldn't stop staring.

Matthew's eyes darkened. He cupped her cheek. "What?" His deep voice was just a murmur. Attraction hung in the air. Reflections cast by the flickering flames in the darkened room changed the shadows on the side of Matthew's face.

April held her breath. If she said nothing, if she leaned forward he would kiss her. Part of her wanted him to more than anything.

He leaned in. "You have milk on your top lip." She pulled back.

"Ah." He wiped his lip. "Milk moustache, huh?"

She breathed out. Tried for casual to lighten the moment. "It's a good look on you."

He took another deliberate drink, letting the foam cover his lip again. "Sexy?" he murmured. His fingers smoothed over her soft skin, then slid into her hair. His gaze held hers as he swiped the foam away with his tongue, leaving his mouth clear.

April swallowed. Yes, it was sexy. He was beyond sexy. Taking what she wanted, what she needed couldn't be bad—anyone could forgive her under the circumstances. Her chin tilted up.

His hand cupped the back of her head, bringing her closer. Her eyelids fluttered closed a moment before his lips met hers.

She'd needed comfort. The touch of his mouth against hers gave a lot more. Maybe it was because of all the men in the world, he was the one she couldn't have. Maybe it was something different. As her mouth opened and their tongues tangled, she gave up wondering and just let herself feel. She breathed him in with every exhale, the scent of citrus, vetiver maybe, mixed with man. He held her face so tenderly her heart melted.

She wanted to touch him, had to touch him. Her hands lifted from her lap to his chest, sliding over the soft cotton of his tee shirt to the warm skin of his neck, then up to his jawline. There was a trace of stubble beneath her questing fingertips,

The kiss intensified. Sitting close to him with her head twisted to his was unsatisfying, not close enough. April wanted to stand up and climb onto his lap, to press her chest against his, to feel his corded thighs beneath her. God, the man could kiss. A knot dissolved in her stomach as his mouth's ministrations, flooding heat downwards. Her body was on fire, desperate for him.

Her hand slid into his hair, and she tugged him closer, leaning back. Encouraging him to lie on top of her.

Matthew pulled his mouth from hers, breathing heavily. "I'm sorry—I shouldn't have." Desire burned in his eyes.

It would be easy to let him take the blame. Easy, but cowardly.

April's breath shuddered in and out as she struggled for air. She pulled her hands back, but he caught them in his.

"April, I…"

"I wanted you to kiss me." There was no denying the truth. "I still want it."

"You're upset." Just that easily, he handed her a get-out-of-jail-free card. His hands squeezed hers. "Worried about everything." He shifted back on the sofa, increasing the space between them. "Tomorrow we'll get everything sorted out. You can move in here."

"Just because I wanted to kiss you, doesn't mean…"

"I know it doesn't." He stood and walked to the fire. "We should just put this…" he waved a hand backward and forward between them, "down to a moment of madness. A moment that won't be repeated. I own this entire building and the upper two floors aren't furnished. There is plenty of room to store your stuff, and you can set up your workshop on the third floor to remake your damaged collection."

"I can't."

"You can." He walked over and stood before her. "What other choice do you have?"

*****

Matthew woke early, scrawled April a note, and decided that rather than run the risk of meeting up with her over the breakfast table, he'd go into work early and stop in for breakfast on the way.

He sat in the diner in front of an Irish breakfast with a large mug of tea, and stared out of the window. When he'd taken her to dinner he'd been ready for her to try and bring up the wedding again, but she hadn't. Being with her brought back memories of the friendship they'd had when she was just a kid. In a lot of ways he wished it could have stayed like that, it would be a lot less complicated. Instead, he'd been captivated by the small dent appearing in her cheek every time she smiled. The plain black dress she wore shouldn't have made his pulse race, but the wide belt had emphasized her waist, and the curve of her hips in a way impossible to ignore.

Later, at her apartment, the way she'd kept her feelings in check so as to deal with the disaster had been beyond impressive. If only she hadn't changed into the damned onesie.

With a sigh, Matthew swallowed the dregs of his tea. She'd looked so cute, so vulnerable, he hadn't been able to resist. The moment their lips met, an overwhelming need had come out of nowhere, blindsiding him. The absolute last thing he needed in his life was an entanglement with June's sister. But with her living in his house, how could he avoid it?

*****

The following morning, April rang around to find a solution. Marie had offered her sofa, but nowhere to store her collection, never mind room to work on it. Calling Eliza was difficult with her fingers crossed, but she managed it.

After a few minutes explanation, she popped the question. "I need somewhere to stay."

"You're welcome to come to me," Eliza said. "But you know I have workmen taking up the floor in the spare room."

Damn. She'd forgotten all about the dry rot rampaging through Eliza's flat like a forest fire.

"I could put you up on the sofa, but all the furniture from the spare room is in there, so you'd have to squeeze in between the wardrobe and the wall."

"I forgot." April wracked her brain for other alternatives and came up empty. There were places she could rent, but without a job her finances wouldn't run to a regular rent check. "Thanks, honey. I'll work something out."

It looked as if Matthew had been right. She had no choices.

She'd called her friends early before they left for work. Hunger gnawed a hole in her stomach, so she padded downstairs.

There was a note propped up on the coffee machine. In

it, Matthew again offered his home. She slotted a couple of pieces of bread in the toaster and sat down to brood.

She'd have to stay with Matthew.

The compulsion to kiss him yesterday had been building all evening. The intense way he looked at her, the way his mouth curved when they were flirting, the way his broad shoulders filled out his white shirt, all had combined in a slow burn she'd had no hope of extinguishing once passion ignited.

He'd given her an easy out by brushing away the kiss as an aberration. When he'd said it wouldn't happen again, the primary emotion she'd felt was regret rather than relief. She didn't trust herself around him. Living with him could very well be dangerous, not because of anything he might do, but because of what she might.

April tucked her hair behind her ears. She needed to think about June.

Whatever money she had managed to save would have to go toward material to remake her collection. She hadn't bought the material for June's wedding dress yet, she'd ordered it, but now she wouldn't have the money to pay.

She straightened her spine and rang her sister.

"Hey! How are you?" June's breezy tones chipped through April's defenses.

"Pretty awful, actually. There was a fire last night in the coffee shop." There was no point in sugar-coating the situation. "The apartment was damaged. This morning I'm homeless and jobless."

"Oh no! My dress…"

June's first thought was about was her dress. No questions about where April was living, how she'd make ends meet…

"The toile is intact, and I'm waiting for the silk to come in, everything is okay with your dress." *Apart from the fact I can't pay for the material.*

"Oh that's great." There was silence for a moment. "You'll get another job easily though, right? After all there must be a million coffee shops in London."

"The thing is, June, I can't pay for the silk." April held her breath, hoping June wouldn't make her beg. "I have to remake my collection, it was smoke damaged."

"Oh." There was a chill in June's voice. "Oh, so you want me…"

"I need you to buy the material."

"How much is it?" She'd never asked how much the material she'd insisted on was when April was paying. Irritation niggled. April pulled out her black notebook, unwrapped the elastic holding the pages in place, and searched it for the dress costings.

When she revealed the price, June gasped. "Wow, it's really expensive."

"Yes, it is." She was buying the material at cost. If June had asked any other designer to make her dress, there was no way she'd be able to get it so cheap. "The best thing would be if you could transfer the money into my bank account. They'll need to be paid next week."

"My cash flow…"

June was making excuses?

"I can't buy it," April said. "I have lost my flat, my job, and my collection has been smoke damaged. As it is, I'm going to have to buy more material for my collection, not to mention…"

"Fine. Fine." June spoke quickly. "I'll get the money from Dad or Michael. You'll have to give me a few days though. I hadn't budgeted for this."

Neither had I. The thought burned through April's mind. *I hadn't budgeted for having to refinance my entire life in an instant.*

"Good. I'll email you my bank details."

"Do that," June said in a tone so harsh she might as well have said the very opposite. "Listen, I have to go. I'll talk to you next week." She hung up.

April felt as though she'd been shot full of anesthetic. Her senses were dulled as though her head was full of cotton wool, and her heart ached as if someone had removed it from her chest and pounded it with a hammer. Not once had June offered help or showed concern for April's plight. She'd meant to tell June about how she'd met up with Matthew, about how he'd offered her somewhere to stay. But June was plainly not interested.

For the first time, the complaints her friends had voiced about her sister's selfishness rang true.

Chapter Six

April was sitting at the kitchen table nursing a mug of coffee when Matthew walked in.

"You're up early." For the past week she'd still been asleep when he left for work.

She jabbed at the newspaper open in front of her with a pen. Some of the small ads were circled. "This morning, I'm looking for a job." Her mouth twisted in a strangled semblance of a smile. "I need to make a contribution to the household."

"What have you got so far?" He pulled up a chair.

"There are a few places looking for baristas."

He reached for the page and scanned it. "All of these are looking for full-time. And there's nothing local. Can you spare the time? I thought you needed to remake everything."

She chewed on her bottom lip. "I do. I can work at night though. I'll try and keep the noise to a minimum."

For the past couple of nights the steady hum of the sewing machine had filled the silent house. She'd purchased all the material she'd need, but rather than farm out the manufacturing to a seamstress, had been carefully remaking each piece of the collection. He didn't know why she wasn't

SALLY CLEMENTS

getting help, but suspected it came down to finances. She was obviously broke.

"You're crazy." He leaned back in the chair and crossed his arms. "I have a solution."

Her head tilted and her eyes narrowed.

"You can work for me."

April shook her head. "I don't know anything about your business."

"You do know how to cook, though, don't you?"

"Matthew…"

He held out a hand palm flat to silence her.

"I contacted an agency last week looking for a housekeeper, and they haven't come up with any candidates yet." The lie tripped easily off his tongue. The thought of some stranger spending all her time in his house while he was out of it wasn't something he would ever contemplate, but April didn't need to know that.

"You need a job, and I need some help around here." He spoke fast to convince her before she threw up more roadblocks. "Every night when I get home I'm too exhausted to even work out what I want to eat. And I have to wrangle the laundry and keep this place clean. I eat out every night because I can't find the time to shop and cook." He leaned forward. "You can drive, can't you?"

She nodded.

"You could take the car today, fill up the fridge, and help me out. I could pay you. It wouldn't be much but…"

"I'd be happy to cook for you anyway, and of course I'd help you out, you don't need to pay."

He held her gaze. "I don't want you to have to go and work in a coffee shop to make money when you could make the same amount by working for me, and cut down the amount of time travelling. You'd be able to get on with the collection." She was weakening; he could see it in her eyes. He pulled out his wallet and withdrew a bundle of notes. "It's only for a month or so, until you have your collection finished. I'm so busy with the Albios launch, you don't want me to starve and have no clean clothes to wear, do you?"

Her mouth curved in a slow smile. "So, cleaning, doing laundry, shopping and cooking dinner," she said. She reached out a hand to his. "Deal."

There was absolutely no reason why the feel of her warm palm against his should send a rush of electricity up his arm. He reached for the car keys from the middle of the table. "I'll catch a cab…"

"I can drop you off and then go on to the shop. And I can pick you up later."

His employees would have a field day with a woman dropping him to the office. "No need." He pressed the keys into her hand. "I'll see you later."

*****

April didn't want to rely on anyone. Independence was one of the reasons she'd worked all the way through college and after it as well, even though her father had always tried to foist money on her. Right now she didn't have a choice in the matter. Matthew was right, trekking out to work every day would take away from the time she had to spend on remaking her collection. And until Elizabeth's insurance company paid out, she had no money to pay rent on somewhere new.

Matthew needed her and was prepared to pay for her services.

There was something immensely satisfying about attacking a list of tasks and ticking them off, one by one.

Shopping? Check. Dinner prepared? Check. Laundry done? Check. After a mop of the kitchen floor and a quick vacuum around the living room the rest of the day would be hers.

She'd dusted every inch of the living room, found homes for all the DVDs that had escaped their boxes, and stacked them in alphabetical order on the shelves. He had an unhealthy fixation with disaster movies.

Rooting around behind the cushions on the sofa had yielded a small fortune in change and long lost pens, and she'd rescued a jam-jar from the kitchen to stack them in. At least the laundry had made it as far as the hamper, or at least most of it had. Presumably firing dirty washing at the basketball hoop directly above the hamper was fun, and picking up the miss-shots less so.

Now she had the house in some sort of order, maintaining it would be easy.

She picked up the old newspapers stacked on the shelf beneath the coffee table to consign to the recycle bin, and shoved them into a large paper bag from an exclusive man's shop.

Her cell phone rang. April glanced at the display.

"Hi Dad." She settled down on the sofa and pulled her legs up. "How's it going?"

"I should be asking you that." Jack Leigh's voice was serious. "When were you going to tell me about your apartment? I had to hear it from your sister."

"I didn't want to worry you."

"She says you've lost your job."

"I lived above my job, Dad," she explained. "It was a two-for-one strike."

"So you have nowhere to live, and no job." He sounded exasperated. "Don't you think this is something I should know about?"

"There's not much you can do." She pulled in a deep breath.

"I can send some money. Help you get back on your feet. June rang me to ask for money to buy fabric for her wedding dress. She told me you're broke and can't afford to buy it." A pause. "Do I gather your sister wasn't paying for the dress?"

"I wanted to make it for her, Dad."

He made the teeth-sucking noise again. "You volunteered to cover all the costs too?"

There hadn't been much volunteering about it. June had presumed April would cover all the costs and it had seemed petty to ask for money, before now.

"She..."

"You're a student, for God's sake. Trying to make your way in the world without help. I admire that about you, honey, but your sister should at least have covered the costs of materials. She should be paying you for your time too, but I guess there's no way June would even think about that." It was the first time she'd ever heard Dad criticize June. "I want your bank details so I can do a transfer today to cover the material. I'll add something to cover the rest of the supplies too. You shouldn't be expected to pay for her dress. Now tell me, what do you need? Have you found somewhere else to live?"

"I'm staying with a friend for the moment." With luck, he wouldn't want to know exactly who. "I've found a temporary job. I've been able to work on remaking my collection."

"Your collection is damaged?" Her father's voice rose. "Your sister didn't mention... "

"Everything is under control. I'm sorted. It's going to take a lot of work but I'm on top of it."

"I'm flying to Dublin in a couple of weeks. June wants to show me the wedding venue." To April's relief he sounded calmer. "I'll spend a few days there and then fly over to see you."

A bead of sweat trickled down April's spine. If he came to London, he'd find out exactly where—exactly who… "There's no need. And I'm so busy at the moment I won't have much time to be with you."

"I'll call when I have the tickets booked." There was no arguing with Jack in this mood. "Now, be a dear and give me your bank details."

*****

As the front door swung open, the smell of something delicious wafted through the air. He should have called, should have told her he wouldn't make it for dinner tonight.

Matthew glanced at his watch. Four o'clock. Just enough time for a quick shower and to change before the meeting with the Albios people. Even though they were interested, there were other players in the game, and tonight would be a chance to make a personal impression over dinner. There was no way to get out of it. Hopefully April would understand.

He checked the spotless kitchen, and glanced into the living room which was transformed from its usual messiness. The wooden furniture gleamed, and she'd even tidied up the DVDs. He peered closer—wow, she'd even alphabetized them. He'd reckoned tales of people arranging stuff in alphabetic order was an urban legend, but apparently not.

As he climbed the stairs a low buzzing came from the

floor above. She must be working on her collection. There'd be time enough to talk after his shower.

The knowledge April was upstairs inhibited him from his usual sing-in-the-shower-fest. He loved belting away songs under the spray, but had been told often enough by his family his enthusiasm didn't make up for the inability to hold a tune. Instead, he washed his hair, then ramped the spray up to full and rotated his shoulders under the hot steam.

There was a shocked gasp.

Matthew's head swiveled, and through the transparent glass shower enclosure, saw a pair of shocked blue eyes.

"Oh, I'm sorry, I didn't know…" Her face was beet-red as her gaze flickered the length of his naked form and back to his face. "I—" She turned on her heel and fled as though pursued by a serial killer.

He'd been thinking about business, but the moment he'd seen her standing in the bathroom his treacherous body had instantly reacted. With a curse, Matthew rotated the dial to cold and stood under the frigid spray until his erection subsided. It took a lot longer than he'd hoped. In fact, his reaction to her was so extreme he had to think of erection-killer things before he felt confident enough to step out and wrap himself in a towel.

"April?" She was nowhere in sight, but at his call she peeked around his bedroom door.

"I'm sorry. I thought there was an intruder." She was staring at the floor.

"It's not your fault. I had to come home early to change."

Her gaze lifted, tracking up his half-naked body in a way that made his mouth dry.

"I smelled dinner." He felt such a heel, she'd cooked, and he'd… "I'm sorry, I should have called but I have a business dinner tonight."

"It's okay. It will taste even better tomorrow." A faint smile flirted with the corner of her mouth.

"You have it." He wished her damned dimple wasn't so inviting.

"I made lots. If you're not going to be here tonight, maybe I'll have a couple of friends around."

Relief flooded through him. Instead of being disappointed, she'd turned the situation around. "Good idea." He walked to the clothes he'd laid out on the bed. "Don't wait up for me, I'll probably be late."

She nodded. "I'll let you get dressed."

Living with April was killing him.

*****

Marie and Eliza were dying to get together, so she'd worked hard all afternoon, made herself a quick omelet, shoved the stroganoff in the fridge, and flicked on the fire for some instant ambience.

She was tugging the floor-length curtains closed as the doorbell rang.

Both her friends stood on the doorstep clutching a variety of goodies.

"We brought margaritas." Marie clutched a couple of silver bottles of premade cocktails.

"And tortilla chips." Eliza hoisted a plastic bag high. She peered behind April. "Where's hunky Matthew?" Her eyes were wild and her eyebrows waggled up and down.

April laughed. "I told you, he's out for the evening."

Eliza's painted lips turned down. "Aw, I thought maybe he'd have come back early."

"Sorry. Girls only. Come on, we'll get glasses." She strode into the kitchen with her two friends trailing after her. They stopped again and again on the route, admiring the pictures, the carpets, the furniture.

"Jeez, you'd think you guys hadn't ever seen a house before," she teased.

"This is no ordinary house." Marie picked a large bowl from the shelf in the kitchen and unleashing a tortilla wave into it. "Matthew must be loaded. Look at all this stuff."

She'd never had Matthew down as a nester, but he obviously was. His house was beautifully put together, and she would bet her lunch money he hadn't had any help from a decorator. "Let's get cozy."

Eliza sighed. "Wow, this is gorgeous." She set down the drinks on the coffee table, then sank on one of the sofas. "So, tell me. How are you getting along?"

Where to begin? She'd told them both the news on the phone. That she'd moved in for a month, that he'd given her a job. She hadn't told anyone about the kiss, somehow it was too personal to share. Especially when her thoughts were so conflicted about it. "He's nice."

"He's nice?" Eliza's gaze sharpened.

"Nice?" Marie echoed.

"He's a nice guy." Sure, she sounded defensive. After all it wasn't every day she backed right down from calling a man a complete heel and in fact did a complete about face. "He's kind, and generous. He came to my rescue immediately, he…"

"He's a knight in shining armor?" Marie leered. "Does he kiss well too?"

A flush heated April's face instantly. *Oh great, facial semaphore.*

Marie's eyes widened. "OMG, he *has* kissed you!"

There was no point in denying it. Not for the first time, she wished she was a better liar.

"Has he?" Eliza asked.

They perched on the sofas awaiting her answer, like buzzards watching the last dying breaths of a wounded gazelle.

"Oh, fine. We kissed."

"When?"

"Where?"

"The first night." Before she had a chance to say more, Eliza was in interrogation mode.

"At the restaurant? When you were wearing that knockout dress?" She sighed, drowning in a sea of romance.

"Right here, after the fire. I was wearing a onesie with ducks on it." She giggled, remembering the ridiculousness of it. "And we were drinking cocoa."

"You've got to admire a man who kisses a woman over cocoa," Marie sipped her drink. "Especially if she's wearing a onesie."

"I can't see it." Eliza's forehead pleated. "I thought it was black for winter, white for summer. I've never seen you in anything with yellow on it, especially not ducks. Don't get me wrong though, I've nothing against ducky onesies."

"It wasn't mine, you idiot."

"If you tell me it was his, you'll totally ruin the moment. You know that, right?" Marie said.

"It's his sister's. All my stuff was in the washing machine, I borrowed it." She tucked her legs under her and refilled her glass. "It was just one of those things, you know, the fire—I was upset…"

"So it was a chaste comforting kiss, was it?" Eliza leaned

forward.

Red flags signaled nope on April's face again. "Um…"

"Just stop beating about the bush and out with it. Every single detail," Marie demanded. "You know you want to."

The feelings dammed up within needed an outlet. April breathed in deep, and recounted the story of the kiss. "And then today he came home early and I caught him in the shower."

The sound emanating from Marie could only be described as a squeal.

"Behind an opaque shower-curtain catch?"

"More like behind a totally transparent shower screen catch." Heat flared though her entire body at the memory. Matthew was gorgeous fully dressed, but naked… She pulled the neckline of her tee-shirt away from her neck. She hadn't been able to tear her gaze away from his spectacular body, had just stood there ogling him and stuttering like an idiot. And when he'd called her back into his room it hadn't been much better. The wanton urge to walk over and run her hands up his broad, damp chest had been so powerful her legs had gone all trembly. It had taken all her composure to act unaffected.

"The thing is, he's *Matthew*." Words were inadequate but she soldiered on. "I mean, he's *the* Matthew, June's Matthew."

"He hasn't been June's Matthew for years," Eliza said.

Marie nodded. "The past is past. Everyone deserves a second chance."

Eliza held her glass up. Clinked it against April's. "Here's to second chances."

Chapter Seven

He'd rapped on her door on the way downstairs, and called, "Breakfast in ten!"

A sound easily mistaken for the growl of an angry bear had sounded from behind the closed door.

Ten minutes had come and gone. The bacon and sausages were keeping warm under the grill, and the fried eggs were in danger of becoming rubber Frisbees. Matthew took the two plates he had warming out of the oven and placed the dish of sausages and bacon on the table. He was sliding an egg onto each plate as the door to the kitchen opened.

April's usual smooth hair stuck up all over the place. She was wearing a short nightgown, and to his eternal relief, sweatpants under it.

"Sunglasses are an unusual look for breakfast time."

She mumbled something, made it as far as the table, and reached for the glass of orange juice.

"Tough night?"

"I went sort of overboard." She swallowed a mouthful of orange juice. Tipped the sunglasses down to reveal tired eyes. "Margaritas are actually very strong."

He grinned. "There should be a health warning." He placed the jug of coffee in the center of the table on the tile with an elephant on it Amy had given him for Christmas. "Cheer up. Breakfast will see you right."

She ate in silence. Then after a few minutes, slipped the glasses off.

He didn't think he'd seen anyone look so wretched in his life.

"How did your meeting go last night?"

"Well, it obviously wasn't as fun as yours." He buttered a piece of toast and handed it over. "But I think it went well." The all-female group from the Albios women's department had a feminine dynamic that had been difficult to deal with. They flirted constantly with him, but frowned at any hint of flirt back. "The clients have agreed to come out today to see us in action."

April frowned. One side of her mouth lifted in a move not seen since Elvis.

"Once they see the ads working, I reckon it's in the bag."

"That's today?" Her voice was just above a whisper.

"We have to go in about…" he consulted his watch, "twenty minutes. You didn't forget, did you?"

"No…no, of course not, I'm just half asleep. I better get a move on." With a teeth-baring smile, she drank her coffee, and picked up the half-eaten piece of toast from her plate. "I'll get dressed."

He'd told her twenty minutes, but in fact, they didn't have to leave for forty-five. So when April walked down the stairs thirty minutes later, they were right on schedule. She'd tied her hair up in a neat ponytail, and was dressed in a tracksuit and sneakers.

"Is everything you own black?"

She shot him a glare, even though his tone hadn't been remotely sarcastic. "No, I also have white clothes."

"I haven't seen any of those."

"That's because it's not summer," she said as though explaining to a troublesome small child. "I wear white in the summer."

"You used to wear all sorts of colors." A memory of April in a green sweater and jeans popped into his head from nowhere. "I remember a green jumper..."

"Yeah, well." She took her coat from the hook and slipped one arm into it. "That was then."

He moved close, and held up the back of her coat so she could slip her other arm in. Her hair smelled of lemon shampoo. The same shampoo he used, so the scent really shouldn't be so enticing. The curve of her ear, the way her hair curled against the back of her neck... "I think you'd look great in red."

Her head jerked as her face turned to his. A trace of pink flushed her cheekbones. "I thought we were late." She stepped away.

Just in time.

*****

There were a lot of cars parked at the airfield, and about thirty people waiting as they arrived.

Like her, they didn't look like runners, the majority dressed in casual clothes rather than custom running kit. So these were the people Matthew worked with. April watched as they approached with smiles on their faces.

"Hi boss." The stranger was very good looking, and obviously single, if the gang of women surrounding him was any indication. He eyed her with interest.

Picking up on the unspoken question, Matthew made

introductions. "Jason, this is April." He introduced the rest as they approached, but there were too many names for April to remember them all.

"Come on over, and Janice will set you up."

Nerves fluttered in April's stomach.

After attaching a tag to her shoelaces, April listened carefully as Janice explained how the system worked. From the corner of her eye, April could see Matthew talking to three women. They were obviously the clients, dressed in business clothes with high heels, rather than casual running gear. "Susan, Matthew's secretary, will be cheering you on." Janice waved across the runway to a blonde woman standing alone in front of a camera. "It all gets rather competitive, I'm afraid."

April swallowed. "I'm not a very good runner," she confessed.

"Don't worry about it. No pressure." Janice grinned. "I'm glad I got the opportunity to record things rather than running though. Of course, Matthew leads the field, but doesn't he always?" She looked curious. "So, you're a friend of his?"

"I'm staying with him at the moment." She didn't want anyone to get the wrong idea, and was on the point of explaining in more detail just why she was living with him when Matthew waved her over. "Ah—"

"Better not keep him waiting." Janice patted her arm, and turned back to the computer set up on the trestle table. "I'll see you later, have fun."

Fun? Hardly. She'd be happy if she managed to manage the run without embarrassing herself by collapsing. The looping track looked considerably more daunting than she'd expected. It seemed to go on forever. April breathed in deep and walked over to Matthew and the clients.

"April, I'd like to introduce Angela, Mel and Belinda."
She shook hands.

"I'm so glad to meet you, April." Angela was obviously
the boss; the others stood silently smiling as she spoke.
"Matthew should have brought you to dinner with us."

They obviously had got the wrong idea about her and
Matthew's relationship too. April wasn't sure what to say.
He's not my boyfriend, would sound gauche.

"April had some friends over last night." Matthew's
words did nothing to explain things.

She cast a glance his direction.

"Well I hope you will join us tonight. It's our last night
in town, and we've persuaded Matthew to have dinner with
us again." The way Angela asked, it was difficult to say no.

"Oh, well, yes."

Matthew looked over to where the rest of his employees
were lining up on the starting line. "I think they're ready to
go. Angela, why don't you all join Janice? She'll show you
how the system works, and you can watch the campaign
over the monitors."

"Wonderful." The clients were obviously impressed.

April was too. The whole office had turned out on a
Saturday to demonstrate the system revealing that
Matthew's employees were really engaged with the whole
process. The smiles and easy way everyone talked around
him couldn't be faked. He must be good to work for.

A hand grasped her elbow. "Let's go." His wide smile
took her breath away. "I'm going to run fast. Don't try to
keep up."

April snorted. "Don't worry."

"Jason's very competitive."

Jason's not the only one.

"Just run at your own pace. Did Janice tell you Susan is acting as our cheerleader?"

They lined up with the others at the starting line. She nodded. "Matthew, I think we should tell the client we're not..."

Someone blew a whistle, and before she had a chance to finish the sentence, they were off. Matthew's long legs propelled him away from her as though he had a rocket strapped to his back. For a moment, she almost stopped dead just to watch the beauty of a man built to run, doing what he did best, but standing staring at him as he did his best impression of poetry in motion would have been a dead giveaway, so she jogged after him.

One by one, the rest of the staff passed her. This was going to be embarrassing.

A slightly overweight redhead jogged along with her. "Oh, this is awful," the redhead groaned.

"Yes, it sure is." April couldn't hold back a smile. "I'm April."

"I know. I'm Margie." The redhead held out a hand. "Accounts."

April shook it. "I don't suppose you know a shortcut," she said in a stage whisper.

"There's no shortcut." Margie smiled. "Just do me a favor, will you? Let me know if my make-up slides off my face or I start getting sweaty." Her gaze was glued to a tall figure in front. "If Jason hadn't suggested drinks after, I'd still be at home in bed."

"Oh, you and Jason?" April waggled her eyebrows.

"Me, Jason, and the rest of the single females from the office," Margie confessed. "But if you're not in, you can't win, right?"

"Right."

"My aim is just to get around this course without falling flat on my face or having a heart attack. I have my sleeves stuffed with tissues, and emergency mascara in my car."

Margie was fun. Talking to her was so distracting April was almost able to block out the ache in her calves as she pounded the asphalt. "I'll let you know if you suffer a make-up malfunction."

Margie gave April a thumbs-up. "I'll do the same for you." She gestured ahead. "Aha, here comes the first screen."

April slowed her pace, allowing Margie to edge further ahead. The screen was filled with a graphic that changed to live feed from the cameras. Two of Margie's friends jumped up and down, waving banners. Seeing them, Margie laughed out loud.

The boost she'd received was evident. Margie's posture changed, as though her body had become lighter and she picked up the pace and ran faster, talking into the recorder hanging around her neck as she did so.

As April approached, the image on screen shifted with a message for her. A stranger, who must be Susan, waved at the camera, and held out a sign proclaiming "You can do it."

The response on April wasn't quite as profound. After all she didn't have friends or family supporting her, but still the encouragement on Susan's face triggered a burst of enthusiasm for the task ahead. Instead of thinking about the whole circuit, she should focus on reaching the next sign. She'd worry about the next one when she got there. Four signs and she'd be finished. The on-screen Susan gave her a thumbs-up, and in response April kept going, lengthening her stride to catch up with Margie.

April fiddled with the device around her neck and carefully recorded her feelings as she ran.

Where's Matthew? April glanced across the track to see him speeding past the final screen. By the time she reached the next one, he'd be finished. She pounded the asphalt automatically. The burn in her legs had ceased to be so painful as her body became accustomed to the steady rhythm, and she concentrated on breathing in and out through her mouth. This wasn't so bad.

She drew level with Margie. "How are you doing?"

Margie's face was flushed, but she was not in any difficulty. "Not too bad. We're not last, anyway."

Sure enough, there were about ten people behind them. Some were red-faced and puffing. Others were walking.

As they approached the next screen, there was a loud shout from across the track. Matthew had his arms in the air, and a moment later, Jason followed.

"The boss always wins," Margie said. "Jason has been training hard all week. He was determined to pass him today."

"So there's a lot of rivalry in the office."

"There is between Matthew and Jason, they're both alpha to the max. Jason's always trying to beat him in something. We have a table-tennis tournament in the summer. Matthew is the unbeaten champion too."

The image of Margie's friends onscreen had showed them waving ten pound notes in the air and squealing. "Lots of people bet on Jason today, but we all bet on Matthew. We knew he hadn't been training as hard because he'd been out at a lot of meetings and working till late, but I knew he'd nail it."

Her gaze was full of questions. "He hadn't been training in the evenings secretly, has he?"

"No. He hasn't been out running since last week." The moment the words left April's mouth she wished she could catch them back. She only knew Matthew's movements because they were sharing a house. Margie would get the wrong idea...

"Have you known Matthew long?"

"For years," she confirmed. "We just caught up again a few weeks ago. I've been staying with him."

"So do you normally live in London?" Margie smiled. "I hope I'm not being too nosy."

April shook her head. Talking was keeping her focused, and the time was flying. They were nearly at the third screen. "There was a fire in the coffee shop under my apartment. Matthew offered me somewhere to stay."

It was evident from the look of disappointment on Margie's face that April's words had shattered some dream she was having about her hard-working boss having a hot affair.

"He's great. When Susan's husband left her last year she fell to pieces," she confided. "She sent out the wrong paperwork and almost scuppered a big contract. Luckily Matthew managed to put things right. She told me he refused point blank to accept her resignation and bought tickets for her and the kids to go to New Zealand to visit her family for a couple of weeks. He always comes through in a crisis."

Yet when June had needed him, he ran. The disconnect was jarring.

This time April approached the screen first.

Susan waved, gave the thumbs-up, but this time the

banner was in Matthew's hands. He'd turned it over and scrawled, "Go, April, go!" on it. He was grinning like a fool.

"You're doing great," she read on his lips.

There was something strangely intimate about the message he mouthed just for her. The look in his eyes was one of pride. As if he knew just how unprepared she'd been for this challenge, and admired her for giving it her all. She talked into the recorder, her pace increasing to match the on-screen Albios-clad feet.

Matthew cheered as she crossed the finish line, and handed her a bottle of water. His arm came around her shoulders, and his mouth brushed hers in a quick kiss.

She wouldn't have thought her heart could beat any faster, but it did.

*****

Where is she? They had to leave in an hour, and April hadn't come back from her shopping trip yet. Matthew dressed in a grey suit and stalked into the sitting room. The house was so quiet without her. Even though she spent a lot of time locked away in the room upstairs, he'd become accustomed to the constant hum of the sewing machine. He glanced at the coffee table. The stack of newspapers he kept under there was gone. no doubt tidied up in her recent cleaning. He checked in the cupboard, then went upstairs to see if she'd stacked them in his room, agitation rising.

He should have cut the advertisements out of them, but there had always been something more important to do. And at a pinch, he could order copies of the photographs of his advertising campaigns, but the thought she'd thrown them away without asking made him grind his teeth.

There was the sound of a key turning in the lock in the front door.

April stood on the doorstep, clutching a handful of bags.

"Where did you put my newspapers?"

Her smile disappeared. "What are you talking about?"

"The newspapers on the shelf under the coffee table, where are they?"

"I put them out for recycling."

Matthew swore and stalking into the kitchen, lifting the top of the paper recycling bin. Recycling day was tomorrow. The papers were there. With a sigh of relief he pulled them out. "I need these. They have my ads in."

She glared. "I didn't know."

"If you don't know something, just ask."

"Fine." Her tone conveyed loudly that she didn't think it was fine at all. She was definitely pissed off. "I'm going to get ready."

"We have to leave soon."

She shot a glare his direction. "Like we had to leave soon earlier?"

With a toss of her long brown hair, she left the room.

Loud music blared from her room as she got ready. Fine, she was in a mood. He got it. Matthew gritted his teeth. He was totally within his rights to tell her off.

Half an hour later, he was pacing the room. This evening was important. Important to his business. And work trumped a little hurt feelings every time. His hands were clenched into fists so he deliberately stretched out his fingers.

When she'd crossed the finish line he couldn't resist kissing her. A certain amount of it had been down to the lustful looks Jason had been firing her direction. The office Lothario had every woman in the place chasing him around, but his eyes had shot straight to April like a heat-seeking missile the moment she'd climbed out the car. Never before had Matthew felt the need to brand a girlfriend as his...

Girlfriend? His? Matthew stopped dead and stared at the curtains. Where the hell had that come from? He was helping April out, not dating her.

The whole idea was crazy.

"Are you ready to go?"

He turned to the doorway.

April's dress was more deep-burgundy than red, and reached just above her knee. Long ruby earrings swung from her lobes, brushing her shoulders. High heels showed off acres of leg.

He swallowed. "You look great."

"Thanks." No smile. She slipped on the black velvet coat she was carrying and opened the front door.

He brushed past her and closed it. "Are you sulking?"

April crossed her arms. "I don't appreciate your attitude." The glare she fired at him would melt steel. "I worked very hard cleaning up your house. Sure, I made a mistake, but it was an easy one to make. If you talked to the housekeeper you were going to hire like that, she'd quit."

"You're overreacting."

"No. I'm not. You treat your other employees with courtesy, why not me?"

"Just because I'm paying you doesn't make you my employee."

"Yes, it does."

"No, dammit, it doesn't."

She was a lot more. She was someone who shared his home, someone he couldn't resist the urge to kiss any longer. He stepped close, slipped an arm around her waist.

Her mouth opened on a shocked gasp.

"You're a hell of a lot more than an employee."

Her hands pressed against his chest. "Matthew..."

The moment he kissed her, everything changed. This was no casual brush of the lips like earlier out at the finish line. Her lips parted under his. Her hands snaked up to the back of his neck, fingers tangling in his hair as their mouths fused.

Through a haze of sensation Matthew was dimly aware they should be going, should be driving to the dinner. But making things right with April was a lot more important. Nothing was more vital than showing her how he felt, making sure she understood. When he finally pulled away they were both breathing hard.

"You are the most irritating man on the entire planet," she whispered. "I don't know what you're doing kissing me." She frowned, but her eyes blazed with arousal.

"I'm taking what I want. What we both want." He touched her cheek. "Tell me you don't want this too."

She bit her bottom lip. "Wanting something doesn't mean we can have it." Her eyes clouded. "There are reasons we shouldn't let this go any further. You and I are far from a match made in heaven."

She was right. Sooner or later they'd have to talk about his past, the past so inexorably linked to hers.

"You and June..."

Once again June was messing with his life. "It was a lifetime ago." The urge to confess the truth was strong. If April understood more about what had actually happened between them, the last barrier to a relationship would dissolve. But in the process, he'd destroy the blind faith she had in her sister's goodness. It was a step he wasn't prepared to take. "You and I are the only ones here. June is history. I'm not saying we're destined to end up together, but this attraction is heading only one place, to my bed." He brushed his thumb against her full bottom lip. "Tell me you want it too."

Her eyes darkened. "You know I do."

He leaned in close again. Breathed over her lips, "Let it happen."

Chapter Eight

The evening was multi-layered. On the surface, they greeted Angela, Mel, and Belinda at the restaurant and discussed business. Beneath, undercurrents swirled. With every glance Matthew's direction, April's heartbeat accelerated. The banked heat in his gaze showed he was thinking the same things she was. When the evening's work was done, there was nothing standing between them any longer.

Every casual touch was a prelude to what was to come.

Soulful jazz played in the background. The restaurant Matthew had chosen was perfect. Small tables covered in crisp white linen tablecloths and sparkling silverware were set within the recesses of an old wine cellar, and the clever lighting made each table its own little world. The serving staff was quick and efficient, and before long, everyone was served with their meal.

"I know you must be wondering if we've come to a decision yet, so I'm delighted to tell you we have." Angela smiled. "Your company has won the contract, Matthew."

Matthew's wide grin lit up his face. "Well that calls for champagne." He called the waiter over and ordered a bottle of Veuve Clicquot. "I'm delighted."

Even though Matthew's success was nothing whatsoever to do with her, April shared in his satisfaction. His employees had worked so hard, and she knew how much this contract meant to him.

The waiter arrived at the table and poured the effervescent liquid into shallow champagne glasses.

"I'd like to make a toast." Matthew raised his glass. "To a successful campaign."

They all drank.

"Seeing the system in action was the clincher," Angela confessed. She raised her glass to April. "Especially seeing you, April."

Mel nodded. "We'd run through the simulation, but when we saw the effect the messages had on you, it really rammed home the effectiveness of the advertising."

Confusion fogged April's mind. "I don't understand."

"You're the average runner." Angela's smile was tinged with apology. "I hope you don't mind me saying that. Matthew is obviously a very dedicated runner, but you are the perfect demographic for the women's mini-marathon which will be the first outing for the system. The average runner in that race is one who jogs occasionally. Who feels confident enough about their abilities to attempt a mini-marathon, but might balk at a full one."

"Sounds like me." It was tempting to confess she thought she might not make it at all.

"When you approached the screens, seeing supporters cheering you on had a profound effect."

April remembered how Margie had seemed to stand up straighter and run faster with her friends cheering her on. When she'd seen Matthew she'd experienced a burst of energy and renewed zeal for the finish. "It invigorated me."

"Yes. We saw many instances of runners picking up speed and really enjoying the messages. When we analyzed the feedback from the voice recorders and correlated the time differences between screens...I'm getting bogged down in the details, forgive me." She underscored her words with a wave of her hand. "Essentially we could see the system worked. The way the campaign was designed had a tangible, positive effect on the runners."

Matthew's *Go April Go!* Sign had warmed her heart and kept her legs pumping, but the sight of him waiting for her at the finish-line had been like coming home. When he'd kissed her it felt right. Totally right. She'd never been in the grip of such a strong sexual attraction. Marie and Eliza were always encouraging her to take a chance, to stop over-analyzing everything and get swept away.

It doesn't have to mean anything more than sex.

The next hours dragged. When Matthew left the table to settle the bill, anticipation was tingling through every inch of her body.

Angela leaned close. "When we first met Matthew we didn't realize he was in a relationship," she whispered. "The other advertising agency pitching for the job seemed to have more experience pitching campaigns to women; after all, they were all female." She leaned back and sipped her espresso. "The most profitable product in our company is our women's range. We want a woman-friendly agency." A slight frown pleated her forehead. "And his second in command..."

"Jason?"

She nodded. "Jason seems a player. We were concerned that Matthew might be the same. Using a firm of playboys to promote our product would be against everything we stand for."

If they knew Matthew had run out on his wedding years ago, the consequences could be disastrous. "I've known Matthew for a long time," she said. "And I can assure you he's a decent man."

She really had no idea how many women there had been in the past seven years. June had dated half of Ireland before settling down, and perhaps Matthew had been the same. The thought of Matthew with a bevy of faceless someones made a tight knot clench around her insides.

She glanced up. Matthew was walking toward them. His gaze was fixed on hers, and the look in his eyes made one thing completely clear. One person alone held his interest right now. *It was time to go home.*

*****

April walked before him up the path to the house they shared. The sway of her hips in the warm claret-colored dress mesmerized. The back of her calves, the indent at the back of her knee so smooth, so touchable. Would her skin be warm under his fingers?

She slipped her key into the lock as he came up behind her quick and close. His hand slipped around her waist as he breathed in the scent of her hair. April leaned back, angling her head to the side. A sound somewhere between a moan and sigh rippled from her throat, making him harden instantly.

Matthew's palm was flat against the front door. The moment it opened, she turned, sliding her hands up his jacket and into his hair. This moment had been too long coming. Every moment in the restaurant had been torture; talking business when instead his entire being demanded he get April alone. Now, at last, the moment had come, and he wasn't wasting a single minute.

April obviously had the same thought. Her slender body pressed against his from breast to thigh, and as their mouths met she made that sound again, shredding the last vestige of his control.

Expertly he flipped their positions so her back was against the solid oak door. His hands smoothed over her ribcage, then his hands cupped her beautiful, silk-covered breasts. There was too much fabric between them. In a less than elegant move, he angled his body away a fraction while his mouth stayed exactly where it was, on hers, and shrugged out of his jacket. Her eager hands helped, tugging at his tie, half-strangling him in her fervor.

To get them naked. As soon as possible.

As his shirt followed the path his jacket had taken to the floor, her hands were unbuckling his belt.

How does her dress…?

"The zip is at the side," she murmured, her voice so sexy husky another wave of lust poured through his body.

He lowered the half-length zipper that clinched the dress tight to her waist.

Her breathing hitched.

Slowly, he smoothed both hands over her hips and down her thighs to the hem.

April bit her lip as he gathered the material in his hands and pulled the dress up and off.

Damn, she's beautiful. A sliver of red lace covered her, matching the red lace bra above. There were tiny red bows on the straps and between her pale breasts. Like a present made for unwrapping. "Red underwear?" He sounded as though he'd been crawling through the desert for a couple of weeks.

"I bought it to match the dress."

Because April was all about the details. Where he pulled on whatever was to hand, she planned every aspect of her appearance. She would match her underwear with her dress; it wasn't as if she'd worn red just for him.

Her head tilted to the side, watching him. Her lips rolled together, then relaxed. She glanced down, then peeked up from beneath her lashes. The all-engulfing flame that had brought them to this point flickered.

She was unsure.

Matthew pressed his lips against her palm, feeling a shiver run through her from the point of contact. "Come upstairs with me."

She held his hand. Nodded. Each step up the stairs had an inevitability to it.

Matthew was tormented by conflicting emotions. It would be easy to give in to desire, to obey his body's urgings. He rearranged the bulge pressing against his zipper.

She deserved more. So did he. Words unsaid built a wall between them.

He needed to explain. And yet he remained silent as they walked to the bed. Said nothing as she turned in his arms and fused her mouth to his.

The taste of her mouth. The soft slide of her warm skin against his palms.

She climbed into bed.

He followed. His fingers smoothed over her face, traced her cheekbones and the soft dip of her indented cheek. The last thing he wanted to do was to bring her sister in to this moment.

"You're frowning." Her voice was soft, like the caresses

her fingers were smoothing over his shoulders. "What's wrong?"

"You mean a lot to me."

"I know."

"I want to make love to you."

Her mouth curved in a smile. "I know that too."

"You don't know everything."

She laid her head back on the pillow. "So, tell me."

"You're not going to like it." She was going to hate learning her sainted sister had faults. She might not even believe him. He rubbed her lips with his thumb, watching her eyes change color and her jaw tilt up.

The easy thing to do would be to taste her again. Let his lips follow the curve of her neck.

Life wasn't easy.

He leaned back, putting space between their bodies. Pulled up the sheet to cover the expanse of tempting, milk-white skin. If he was going to do this, he had to block her body from view. "I have to talk to you about the wedding."

Her smile faded. "June's wedding?"

"June's wedding." The moment of total intimacy was fading away.

Her hands left his shoulders.

"June's wedding. First time around."

*****

Well that was a passion-killer.

They were making love, and Matthew was thinking about June?

His words felt like a slap in the face.

April wrapped her arms around herself, holding the sheet he'd pulled up in place. She'd left her dress downstairs; otherwise she'd get out of this bed right now, rather than hear how he still had feelings for her sister.

Of course, it hadn't just been the two of them, had it? There had also been a baby. A baby that would be her niece or nephew if it had lived. And Matthew would be her brother-in-law if he hadn't run.

He'd run.

He'd broken her sister's heart, and he'd run.

"I don't want to be lying here in my underwear talking about you and my sister." He should put some clothes on over his spectacular chest. The thought of June running her fingers over his chest and a whole lot more, made her nauseous. She glanced to the end of the bed, spotting what she wanted. "Could you pass me the robe?"

Silently, he complied.

She scooted up and shoved her arms into it, tugging it closed and belting it. "This was a bad idea." She swung her legs out of bed.

"No." He stopped her with a hand on her arm. "April, I know you don't want to listen, but…"

"Your timing sucks."

"I can't…won't make love to you without talking about this first."

"She's moved on, Matthew. She doesn't want you anymore. I know you might find that difficult to deal with, and maybe you're regretting walking away, but you've had years to make everything right, and now it's too late." April sucked in air.

Why the hell it had to be her who explained this to him, she didn't know. It seemed a particularly cruel handful of cards to be dealt, to have to fall in love with a guy and then tell him his chances with her sister were nil.

Fall in love?

The fastest double-take in history. His dark hair was mussed from her fingers. There was a trace of pink lipstick on the dip of his neck where she'd tasted him. His wide tanned chest tempted her fingers. She wasn't in love with Matthew Logan. She wasn't in love with Matthew Logan.

She wanted sex with Matthew Logan. She liked spending time with Matthew Logan. It wasn't love. Wasn't even close.

He looked pissed off. *Good.* At least she wasn't the only one.

He reached out and grabbed her legs, pulled them back into the bed, and smoothed the sheet over her again. "You can leave once you've heard what I have to say, but not before." His mouth was set in a tight line.

"Your seduction techniques leave a lot to be desired."

"Yeah, tell me about it." He rubbed a hand through his hair. His shoulders slumped as if pressed down by a heavy weight. He leaned his back against the headboard, and pulled the sheet over his abs. "First off, I don't feel anything for June any more. You're the only woman who interests me."

Right.

"I thought she'd come clean. At least to her family, so many years later. I guess I shouldn't blame her, but I do."

"Matthew, this story is an old one."

"You don't know the whole story." His eyes flashed. "You don't know the half of it."

What June had gone through wasn't imagined. She'd been there, had seen the devastation on her sister's face when Matthew left. Whatever spin he tried to put on it, wouldn't change the facts.

She crossed her arms. "So tell me."

Matthew breathed in deep. "I was young, and I thought I loved her. I thought she loved me."

She closed her eyes, hating the pain that stabbed her heart at his words.

"It was a long time ago, and she was my first love. My first lover. We always used protection, so when she became pregnant I was stunned. We both had so many plans for our futures, things we wanted to do before we became parents. I'd like to say I was happy about the prospect of getting married, but I wasn't ready. I wasn't even vaguely ready to settle down."

"So you ran."

"No." He clutched her hand. "I knew the right thing to do was to marry her, so I proposed and she accepted. My future had changed, but I thought it contained her. And our baby."

He'd never spoken about the baby before. April's chest expanded with her held breath.

"I wanted the baby, and when she miscarried..." His mouth twisted. "I was devastated."

"You could have stayed around. There was nothing stopping you."

His gaze locked on hers. He spoke slowly, deliberately. "When June lost the baby she was relieved. She told me now we didn't need to get married after all. She wasn't even sure if I was the father. She'd been sleeping with another two guys while she was going out with me."

April's throat dried. Her heart was pounding fit to burst. He was telling the truth, no-one could fake the pain shadowing his eyes.

"All the preparations for the wedding had been planned, and everyone was ready for us to become husband and wife.

She couldn't tell her parents she'd been sleeping around; they'd already been pushed to the edge with the news she was pregnant."

He looked into her eyes. "June begged me to take the fall, April. She asked me to be the runaway groom, so her reputation would be intact."

"Why didn't you…"

"Tell anyone?"

She nodded.

"Amy overheard a telephone conversation I had with June. She's the only one who knows the truth. I was betrayed and angry, but I still felt enough for her I realized I could weather the storm easier than she could. I had an offer for college in Scotland, and I took it."

Chapter Nine

The foundations of April's world were rocked to the core by Matthew's story. She didn't want to believe June had lied for years, but the emotion in his face hadn't been faked. For the past week, she'd avoided him while she teased out the truth, running over past conversations with June and Amy in her head. Trying to reconcile this new reality.

She'd sewed all day and most of the night for the past week—the good news was her collection was finished, and she'd started working on June's dress. The bad news? That from the moment he came into the house she wanted to go to him.

Somehow she'd stopped seeing Matthew as hot-fling-prospect, and connected deeper. He's shown her a glimpse of his emotions, his past pain, and tangled her feelings for him in the process. She still wanted to jump his bones, but she also wanted to smooth the kinks from his brow.

She didn't want to care, but she couldn't avoid the emotions swirling inside.

She'd always seen life in black and white, but now, everything was dove grey, so for the past four nights April had eaten before he got home and had snuck back upstairs to avoid him, leaving his dinner in the oven. He'd followed a familiar routine since then, had come home then gone out running for an hour before eating.

He'd come home over an hour ago, changed, and gone out again. She'd seen him pounding the sidewalk from her garret window.

If he kept to his routine, he should be back soon from his run.

The phone rang.

"Hello?"

"Uh, hi. Is Matthew there?"

April recognized Amy's voice instantly. "He's out running." She pulled in a deep breath. "That's Amy isn't it? It's April."

"April? *April?* I never expected to hear your voice at Matthew's house."

"I'm staying here. There was a fire at my apartment."

"I-I'm confused. I thought you hated my brother."

April bit her lip. She'd broken off all communication with her friend, had refused to consider any truth apart from the one June was selling. "I did." She sucked in a deep breath. Amy had every right to hate her. Had every reason to tell her to go to hell, but she had to be brave. Had to try to make things right. "I don't hate him anymore. He told me the truth about him and June. I'm sorry, Amy. I should have listened."

She heard Amy's puffed out breath. "I never thought I'd hear you say that."

"June…"

"She never told you?"

April shook her head, even though Amy couldn't see the action. "Even now, she's sticking to her story."

"I don't blame you," Amy's voice was soft. "If it was just a case of believing my brother rather than June I would have believed him blindly too. But I heard June tell him…"

"I know. He told me."

The blinkered love she'd always felt for her sister, her refusal to listen to Amy when she'd told her the break-up hadn't been his fault, churned up feelings that burned deep inside. Just like every other resident of Brookbridge, she'd condemned Matthew without a trial. Sure, June had lied, but the way April had treated him had been worse.

"I've missed your friendship."

April's stomach clenched at Amy's words. "I've missed you too. I don't expect you to forgive me."

"Matthew must have forgiven you if you're staying in his house."

April closed her eyes. He'd more than forgiven her. She'd been angry at him for years, but when his arms held her close and he kissed her hard, she'd been ready to throw all her anger away and drag him upstairs to bed.

He'd put a halt to their lovemaking by insisting on telling her the truth. And she'd punished both of them by avoiding him as a result.

"Is there something going on I should know about?"

"I like Matthew a lot. I guess I always did." There was the sound of singing in the background. "Where are you?"

"Ah. That's why I'm calling. I'm in Guatemala. Here's the number." She reeled off a list of numbers and April quickly wrote them down. "My money was stolen, and I need Matthew to rescue me."

"He should be back soon."

"Get him to call me, would you? I'll wait by the phone."

Moments later Matthew's key turned in the lock. His

footsteps slowed as he walked to the kitchen. "Hi." He stood in the doorway, eyeing her as if waiting for her to run.

"Amy called. She needs help." She crossed the room and pressed Amy's number into his hand. "She's in Guatemala."

He grabbed the phone. "Was she arrested?"

"Her money was stolen."

"Damn." He punched in the number and strode back and forth across the kitchen.

"Amy?" There was urgency in his voice. "Are you alright?" He strode to the table and grabbed the pen. "Tell me where I should wire the money." He wrote down details in a messy scrawl. "Okay, sit tight. I'm on it."

He listened for a moment, quirking an eyebrow at April. "Yes. She's here. Uh-huh. Well I don't know."

Amy was obviously filling him in on their conversation. His gaze heated as it travelled from April's eyes to her mouth. "Maybe. Are you coming home soon?" Whatever she said next made him grin. "Call me from the airport, and I'll pick you up."

Matthew hung up and dialed another number, arranging a money transfer.

April took two steaks from the fridge, and tossed a salad.

He terminated the call and just stood there, staring.

"I hope you're hungry, these steaks are massive." April heart's was pounding so hard, she felt sure he could hear it across the room.

The physical exertion had made him sweat. His hair was messy from the run. His shorts hung low on his hips revealing the bumps of perfect abs.

April's stomach flipped. "I needed some time."

He moved quickly to her side, standing so close she breathed in his distinctive scent and it made her a little crazy.

"I know." His hand touched her waist, then dropped to his side. "I need to shower." An eyebrow rose. "If I do, will you still be here when I get back?"

His stare was so compelling she couldn't look away. "I'll be here."

He traced her cheek with a finger. Gazed at her lips with such intensity that she swayed toward him, wanting the touch of his mouth desperately.

"Give me five." He turned and raced up the stairs.

April lowered herself onto the nearest chair before her legs gave out. The attraction between them was off the charts hot. She was in way over her head, consumed by an uncontrollable desire to forget the past and live in the present. To feel his hands roam over her body and taste his mouth.

She dished up the steaks onto plates as he came down the stairs.

He'd dressed in worn jeans and a sweatshirt that looked so soft her fingers itched to feel. "So you talked to Amy."

"Yes," she whispered, choked with emotion.

"How's work going?" He grabbed a bottle of red wine from the rack and opened it.

"The collection is done." When June's dress was finished, she'd have no reason to stay with him any longer. The thought of leaving tore at her insides. "I just have to make June's dress."

He probably wasn't even aware he frowned at the mention of June.

"I don't want to talk about her." Her words came out as a whisper.

"Me either." He ate quickly. "So, you don't need to work

any more tonight?" His gaze burned everywhere it touched. Her eyes, her mouth, her neck.

"I am taking tonight off." She grinned. The electricity arcing between their bodies was too intense; she desperately needed to lighten the mood. "Maybe we can find a rom-com on Netflix."

Matthew grimaced. "Euww. How about a disaster movie?"

"Maybe both?"

"Sounds good." He finished off the last mouthful of steak. "We could eat dessert in front of the fire."

"What if we don't have dessert?" She'd found out early Matthew was addicted to ice cream, which was unbelievably unfair, considering he didn't have a spare ounce of fat anywhere on his body.

"I'm sure we can find something." He was looking at her mouth again and suddenly the thought of him feasting on her mouth flashed white-hot.

She licked her top lip.

He groaned. "That ties me in knots." He pulled her up from the table. "Every time you lick your damned lip, I want to." His warm breath puffed against her lips, then with one warm lick he did as he'd promised. A bolt of heat flashed from her mouth to her core, making her dampen instantly.

"I don't want to watch TV," he murmured against her lips.

"I don't either." Her lips parted on a sigh.

Kissing her was like being let back into heaven. She'd avoided him every day for the past week, and frustration had forced him out to tire his body by pounding on the streets of London, rather than into April. Every time he'd returned she was working, the sound of the sewing machine humming upstairs behind the closed door.

The night a week ago when he'd spoken about June, she'd climbed out of bed and told him she had to think. He didn't know if she believed him, but she wasn't angry, just distant. He wasn't used to waiting for anything, but he'd had to wait for her to make the first move.

Now she had.

In the bedroom she turned her back and slipped off her clothing, strangely shy.

He stripped off his sweatshirt and shucked his jeans and climbed into bed, stretching out his arm to her. "Come here."

She climbed into bed in her underwear, a blush pinkening her cheeks.

A wave of tenderness engulfed him as he pulled her close to his body, teased his lips over hers. His tongue dipped into her mouth, tasting her. She felt so warm, her skin so soft his body responded to her nearness instantly. He'd wanted her for so long, it felt as though everything before had led up to this moment.

He smoothed down her spine with his fingertips. "I just want to hold you."

She snuggled closer and ran her hands over his shoulders.

Tonight was the first night they'd have together—tonight was for kissing, for building the passion to fever pitch. She groaned into his mouth as his hands rested on the flare of her hips. No matter how much she tempted, tonight was about showing her how much he cared, taking it slow.

The moon shone through his open curtains, bathing her with its pearly glow. The eyes staring into his were dreamy, full of an indefinable emotion.

"Turn around, let's sleep."

She smiled. Turned. And pressed her body close shoulder to toe. His palm flattened against the curve of her stomach, he breathed in the scent of her hair, of her neck.

And held her, as night drifted into dawn.

*****

Sleeping together was becoming a habit. They hadn't made love yet, but the need was becoming too much for both of them. Last night she'd cupped his erection through his boxers, all the while sighing encouragement. He'd almost lost it then and there.

Amy had told him April had apologized for not believing her. She'd told him April's past loyalty was understandable. She'd wanted to know where his relationship with April was going.

He didn't know. April was the only woman he'd ever spent time with who knew everything about his past. The connection between them was deep, the need for her overwhelming. In relationships post June, he'd keep a distance that was impossible with April. He'd started coming home early just to see her smile.

Making love would sail their relationship into dangerous uncharted waters, but holding back was becoming more and more impossible.

He'd taken to walking outside at lunchtime to clear his head. Today, he'd spotted the perfect gift in an antique shop and had impulsively bought it. His fingers clutched around it as she opened the front door before he had a chance to.

"I thought we'd eat early. I've got someone coming

around."

"Who?" They'd been living in a bubble—she'd taken to visiting friends rather than having them around.

"She's a model called Lena. The collection is finished, and she's coming over to try on dresses for me. A sort of dry-run."

April strode into the kitchen and took a casserole out of the oven, and picked baked potatoes from the oven shelf.

"So do you need an audience?"

April looked up in surprise. "Actually it would be good to get a reaction from someone other than me." Her mouth curved in a tentative smile. "Would you mind?"

"Have you ever known a man to turn down the chance of watching models strut their stuff?"

The smile became a full-on grin that filled him with light. "Guys are all dogs."

"Woof."

She laughed. "She'll be here in an hour."

He opened a bottle of wine, and poured two glasses. "I'm looking forward to seeing the collection. You've been working hard." He picked up her hand and examined her fingertips. "There are needle dents in the top of your fingers."

"Tiny badges of honor." Her gaze skittered to the corner of the room. "June's dress is made too."

June. "That's good." Maybe he should leave it there. *No.* "I'm not going to the wedding, you know. I was never going to go to the wedding."

Her gaze met his, eyes wide. "Why did you let me think you would?"

"I didn't want to stop seeing you." The truth flooded out. There was nothing to lose anymore.

Her eyes narrowed. "You were messing with me?"

"I was keeping you here." He brushed a finger over her bottom lip.

Her eyes darkened. "I've been thinking about why she invited you in the first place." She sipped wine.

"Maybe she thought it was time to rehabilitate my reputation."

"She could have done that by telling the truth."

The fact she believed him, that she'd taken the time to think things through, and had realized what he feared she never would, that June wasn't as pure as snow, warmed him. "I guess she's been sticking to one version of events for so long, it would be difficult to switch tracks."

April's mouth set in a firm line. "There's the truth, and there's a lie."

Black and white. With April there were no shades of grey. If her sister wasn't an angel, she must be a devil. "She was young." He didn't want to make excuses for June, but things were never quite so clear-cut. "She made a mistake by not telling you, but I can understand her motivation."

"I can't."

Her shoulders were stiff and unyielding, just like her mind. She pushed the food around on her plate.

"If I'm willing to forgive and forget, you should too."

"You don't have to see her." She dropped the fork, and with it any pretense of eating, and concentrated on her glass instead. "I have to have her here for a fitting. I'll make sure it's when you're out."

He covered her hand with his. "There's no need. We live here together. It's about time she knows that." Now her collection and June's dress were finished, she could move out as she'd always planned. The thought of coming home to an empty house held no appeal, but her departure was inevitable. Just not yet.

"We're not together, Matthew." She didn't move her hand away.

"We are."

Her lips parted.

"I care about you, April. I care about us."

The hand holding her wine wobbled. He took the glass from her fingers. Placed it on the table. And kissed her.

*****

Lena stalked into the sitting-room wearing the final dress in the collection. Well the penultimate dress, the final would be June's wedding dress and it didn't fit Lena. She stepped in a funny model show-pony gait to the fireplace, and twirled on the spot. Then stuck her hip out in typical model pose.

"I love your dresses, they make me feel fierce."

"You look deadly in them," April said. "Thanks so much for coming tonight."

"Oh, hey, you're welcome. The others aren't ready yet, so it's great to wear something I'm actually going to be modeling next month."

"Would you like a drink?" Matthew stood.

Lena raised her hands, palms out. "I can't. I'm meeting my boyfriend." She glanced at her watch. "I'm just going to change and go."

April stood, shot Matthew a quick glance, and followed Lena from the room. There were other elements of the collection to be finalized still, jewelry and hair, but the most important part—the clothes—was now ready.

Exhaustion mixed with relief. She took the final dress and slipped it onto the rack as Lena shimmied into her skinny-jeans.

"So you had to remake the entire collection? That must have been a nightmare."

"It was." The days and endless nights of work had elevated her stress levels to beyond crazy. She'd worried she wouldn't have enough time to get June's dress finished too. After all, the wedding was before the fashion show, but the fashion show had to take precedence. There was too much riding on the show to risk it. Some very influential people had accepted invitations, and if she was lucky, the job of her dreams could come from it.

"Well your stuff rocks." Lena slicked lip-gloss over her perfect lips. "You're very talented."

April's heart swelled. She barely knew Lena, and the praise was unexpected. "That's nice of you to say."

"I mean it." Lena walked to the rack and fingered one dress in particular. "So many of the clothes I model are total fantasies, but these...I can imagine wearing this stuff for real. I like the way they flatter the wearer, and aren't all shock-value, you know?" Her pretty face screwed up. "I can't count the times I've strode the runway with a dress stuck up with tape and my ass hanging out. They're classy and beautifully made."

She grabbed her bag from the bed. "I'd better go."

"Thanks again." April followed her down the stairs.

"Night, Matthew, good to meet you!" Lena called through the open door to the sitting-room.

Matthew called back something.

"He's a keeper." Lena winked. "Have a good night."

Then she was gone. Leaving them alone again. April closed the front door, turned, and leaned against it.

He is a keeper. The fact he'd insisted she hear the truth

about the past before they gave in to the heat blazing between them proved it. And since she'd joined him in his bed he'd been so tender her heart bloomed open like a flower under the sun.

Kissing Matthew, touching him, was so incredibly erotic she daydreamed about being with him all day long, but every night when he turned her around and curled into her back frustration coiled like an anaconda in her stomach.

With every touch, binds curled around her heart. The press of his lips against her hair filled her with light, with foolish hope. Her oft-repeated mantra that love doesn't last was under sensual attack, and she hadn't a clue how to wrestle control back.

The arousal pressing against her every night proved he wanted her just as much as she wanted him. Tonight she wouldn't take no for an answer.

At times like this, April sort of wished she'd had more of a past. She'd never been serious about anyone before, not like this. Sex had been a natural progression to her two previous relationships, but they'd been fun, rather than great romances.

Not that this was a great romance. Not yet.

She sucked in a breath and straightened. Was she going to stand here propped up against the door all night, or go and join him in front of the fire?

No brainer.

He was standing by the fire as she walked in, warming his butt.

"Your dresses are great." He stepped close. "I brought you something." He reached into the pocket of his suit and pulled out a tiny blue box.

She turned the box over and over in her hands. "What

is it?"

"Open it."

She pressed the tiny button and the box sprang open. Inside, a silver filigree thimble nestled in sky-blue silk.

"I thought it might save your fingertips."

April slipped the tiny thimble over her index finger. "It's beautiful."

"I'm glad to see you so happy."

She looked up into his face. "Beyond happy. There's only one thing that will make me happier."

"Oh?" The way his eyebrows rose was so cute, she couldn't resist for one minute longer.

She put the thimble back in the box, and slipped it into his pocket. Stepped up close and personal. Her hands touched his chest, slid up to the nape of his strong neck, and tangled in his hair.

He didn't move. But his eyes darkened.

Up on tiptoe, she pressed her mouth to his. Traced the seam of his lips. Intensified the contact.

Nothing.

She pulled away, stared up into his hooded eyes.

"Are you sure?" His voice was so deep it was almost a growl.

"Yes."

The moment she spoke, his hands rose from his sides and clasped her hips tugging her closer. His mouth lowered to hers, and this time he was fully present. Kissing him was right, was what she wanted, needed, yearned for. His tongue tangled with hers and a blaze of heat turned her blood molten.

His hands slipped under the loose hem of her shirt, slid up her warm back.

The need to have his skin against hers was urgent, so her fingers fumbled to undo the buttons of his shirt. Why were there so many of them?

His mouth lifted from hers a fraction and its corners turned up. "You're growling."

"Shirt. Buttons." Frustration made her frown.

His fingers took up the task, and when it was unfastened he shrugged one shoulder then the other from the shirt and threw it on the floor.

"That's better." Her hands slid over his wide expanse of golden skin, feeling the warmth against her palms.

He removed the rest of her clothing, unfastened his jeans and shrugged them and his boxers off.

The feel of his hands stroking her skin all over was so erotic her legs trembled. It wasn't clear who moved first, maybe they both did, but in moments the soft wool of the fluffy white sheepskin rug tickled her back, while her side warmed from the heat of the fire. Matthew lay over her, his thigh between hers, hands bracketing her head.

His dark brown eyes were almost ebony. Her heart expanded at the look in his eyes.

Warm lips trailed across her mouth, teased her jawline, nuzzled her neck.

"You taste nice."

"Nice?" she murmured. "Only nice?"

He moved lower, licking around her erect nipple, then tasting it. "Like honey and cream."

Squirming was pretty darned unladylike, but she did it anyway, feeling his erection twitch against her upper thigh in response.

He was killing her. Inch by inch as his mouth dusted over her stomach and his fingers stroked over her stomach to the apex of her thighs. She wriggled again.

"Hold still." His warm breath puffed over her and her back arched in ecstasy. He had to be closer, had to be...

His thumb brushed against her sensitive nub effectively obliterating thought.

His name burst from her lips, wrapped in a moan. She was on total sensory overload. The warm wool beneath her, his hot body covering hers, his fingers stroking her inner thighs, encouraging her to open her thighs further. When he tasted her she bit her lip in a vain attempt to keep silent.

It was a losing battle.

His tongue was truly magical, and just when she couldn't hold back any more, he slid one finger, then two into her and transferred his mouth's attention to her nub.

April grasped his shoulders. Her body tingled all over, and her muscles tensed. Her chest rose and fell rapidly as her foot rubbed along the side of Matthew's thigh. The wave of sensation swelled, overwhelming in its power and intensity, crashing over her and dragging her under.

As blood thudded through her veins, Matthew shifted up and lay on his side next to her. His hand stroked up her arm then he pulled her close. She rested her forehead against his, their mouths mere millimeters apart.

The slow movement of his hand over her back was delicious.

Her limbs were heavy and warm satisfaction spread through every inch of her body. Her eyelids drifted closed.

His mouth met hers, firm lips caressing hers slowly and gently.

April breathed in his scent, the warm scent of sandalwood mixed with man. His chest brushed against the tips of her breasts, igniting the flame again.

"Mmm."

His tongue tangled with hers, and the momentary sleepiness dissipated instantly, replaced by a need for more.

Her palm skimmed the powerful muscles of his back, slid down to his rear.

"Hold that thought," he murmured against her lips. He stood and walked to his discarded clothing, snagged a small foil packet from his jeans, and returned to the rug. "We could go upstairs to bed, you know."

She smoothed the soft wool rug with her palm. "Or we could just stay here for a while."

Passion blazed in his dark eyes. Her gaze dipped lower to the hard evidence of his arousal.

Her mouth curved in a sexy smile. "Come on over here."

He didn't have to be told twice, opening the packet and smoothing protection over his erection before joining her.

Every touch, every taste, every moment he wasn't inside her was a torment she couldn't bear. His chest flattened hers, and she angled her legs apart, wrapping them around him. The feel of him at the juncture of her thighs...

"Look at me."

April's eyes opened.

Matthew's expression was so intense it was almost fierce. He kissed her hard, all the time staring into her eyes as he inched carefully into her. Her fingers pressed into his back, urging him on, and at the encouragement, he thrust into her, filling her completely.

The intensity of their coming together physically was dwarfed by the overwhelming intimacy of their inner connection. For the first time ever, this was not just about the physical act, but about something more. The beauty of it, the soul-deep oneness of the two of them made April clutch Matthew closer as the thrusts intensified and quickened.

When the quickening of her orgasm stirred, his did too, bringing them to thunderous climax together.

*****

Matthew woke early and called the office. He'd been putting in many extra hours over the past couple of months; he could afford to take a day off. And after last night, the last thing he felt like was braving the traffic and being closeted in a dark room for the day.

Unless that room was his bedroom—which right now contained a sleeping April.

He poured two cups of coffee and padded back upstairs. Last night had been incredible. The relief of not having lost her had clutched at his throat when she walked to him in the sitting-room with intent in her azure eyes. And when she pressed her lips against his...for a moment his brain-cells had shorted out.

Sex before the fire had been incredible. And when they'd linked hands and climbed the stairs to his bedroom, the thought of sleep had been far from both of their minds. He couldn't get enough of her, and luckily the feeling was mutual. Eventually at about four in the morning their bodies were sated, but then they'd talked. Really talked. Until the shell pink in the sky spearing through the gap between the curtains painted dawn over the sky.

Then she'd turned her back to him, and edged back so every inch of her was pressed against his front, he'd wrapped his arms around her and fallen in a deep, dreamless sleep. Holding April was right. Having her in his bed perfect.

So perfect he wondered what the hell he'd got himself

into.

The sexual tension between them had been so intense, he'd felt sure once they made love the urge would abate, but in fact the opposite was true. He wanted her more than ever.

There was no way on earth April was the one. No way he'd settle down and embrace matrimony with the one person he thought he'd never feel like that for.

It wasn't just the complication of her being June's sister, it was more. The unwillingness to trust wound tight with the reluctance to be made a fool of again and tangled around his insides.

Having her in such close proximity, living in his house, cooking his meals, and being here every time he came home had forced an unreal intimacy. Now they'd added sex into the mix, the intimacy had deepened. Matthew pushed away the memory of staring into her eyes, staring into her soul, as they made love. Something inside had shifted in that moment, as though the wall guarding his heart had crumbled a little.

He didn't like it.

The smart thing would be to help her move out as soon as possible—to shore up his defenses. For the life of him, he couldn't let her go yet. Maybe in a week or two the passion blazing between them would burn out and they could go back to their regular lives.

April sat up as he came into the bedroom, clutching the sheet against her perfect breasts.
Her eyes widened. "I thought you'd left."

"I decided to take the day off." He handed over one cup of coffee, placed his own on the bedside table and climbed back into bed.

A week or two, but until then…

Chapter Ten

Spring was in the air. London's parks filled with daffodils, and light stretched the dark evenings. There was no reason any more to stay in Matthew's house. The collection was finished, and June's dress too. A check had arrived from the insurance company in charge of her claim for the damaged dresses, giving April some wriggle-room, loosening the binds tying her to Matthew.

I don't want to go.

They didn't talk about her moving out. When he came home they kissed with an urgency bordering on desperation and tumbled into bed. She'd become mesmerized by his smile, captivated by his laugh, hungry for his touch.

What was only ever supposed to be an affair had become something more. Something dangerous. Daydreams of her future inevitably included him.

She missed the contact with people in the coffee shop. Missed the ability to have her friends over—somehow inviting them to Matthew's house always felt wrong, especially as he avoided every opportunity to meet them. His house was spotless, and the silent house was beginning to feel like a prison.

April carried another of the chairs out of the kitchen and then pushed the kitchen table into the hall. She'd picked up a bottle of liquid polish on her last visit to the store. Keeping her hands busy was one way of diverting her thoughts, and a thorough mopping of the floor followed by an application of polish would eat up more of the empty hours until Matthew came home.

She had half the floor washed when the phone rang.

"Hi, April. It's Elizabeth."

It seemed like forever since she'd spoken to her landlady and boss. April shoved the mop into the bucket of foamy water and perched on a chair in the hallway. "Hey! How's it going?"

"Good. That's why I called actually. The work is done on The Coffee Haven, and we're almost ready to re-open. I'm calling all the old gang to see if anyone can come back to work. The apartment has been refurbished too, and I wanted to offer you first option on it."

Her old life was right there, at her fingertips.

"I know you may have found somewhere else…"

"Actually…I'm still staying with a friend."

"Having to move out—and the damage to your collection… I wouldn't blame you if you didn't want to move back in." Elizabeth's voice was hesitant. "But if you do I'd like to offer you three months without paying rent. To make up for it."

April wiped her palm against her jeans. "When's the Coffee Haven opening again?"

"The week after next, if I can round up enough staff."

April bit her lip. Matthew didn't need her. Not really. She breathed in. "I'd like to come back to both."

"That's great!"

They finalized the details.

Tonight, when Matthew came home, they'd talk. If she stayed it would be because he'd asked her to. Because there had been a decision made between them to move their relationship to the next level.

The thought of more was frightening. Relationships didn't last, but her feelings for Matthew were all consuming. She couldn't deny them any longer in the hope of avoiding heartache.

Maybe he didn't want more. Maybe sleeping together every night was enough for him, but it wasn't enough for her. She had to have more.

It was tempting to hold on to what they had. To enjoy the moment without rocking the boat. But right now they were like a boat adrift, floating without purpose. She was making a grab for the oars—with luck she wouldn't capsize them in the process.

*****

The house was dark when Matthew came home. He flicked the light on in the hall and frowned. Chairs and the kitchen table blocked the hallway. He dropped his briefcase and then squeezed past them into the dark kitchen.

There was a dark shape slumped in the corner of the room. He fumbled for the switch, flooding the room with light. "April?"

She was huddled in the corner.

"April?" He said louder. Was she hurt?

She stirred. Her head rose and sleepy eyes blinked.

"What are you doing?"

A bottle of liquid sat on the floor before her, and a damp sponge.

"Ah." Her face reddened. She ran her tongue over her

lips. "What time is it?"

"Late."

She reached out and touched the shining floor in front of her. Picked up the bottle and sponge and got to her feet. "I was putting polish on the floor."

"But why are you in the corner?"

She rolled her eyes. "I…"

He finally got it. The reason she looked so damned embarrassed. "You painted yourself into a corner."

Her gaze lifted. She grinned. "I know. It's totally stupid, isn't it? Everyone knows you start at the far reaches and wax in, but I was distracted and before I knew it I'd boxed myself into this corner." She ran a hand through her hair. "I must have fallen asleep waiting for the damned stuff to dry." She held up the bottle. "It takes an hour, apparently."

She stepped forward on fluffy-sock clad feet. "I'll just finish this and start dinner."

Matthew walked into the room and took the polish from her hands. "Forget it. We'll go out." They hadn't left the house for days. With other women, he'd taken them out to dinner and dates but with April they'd fallen into a rut of eating at home like an old married couple.

She reached for the bottle. "It will only take a minute to finish up."

As usual, she was acting the good housekeeper. He hated it. He didn't want her to wait on him, to be responsible for keeping his house in order any more.

"Leave it."

"If I leave it, we'll have to wait even longer to put the furniture back."

"Fine. I'm going upstairs to change."

He stalked away, frustration roiling in his gut. She was

always here. Always waiting. He'd lived alone for so many years; the constant sharing set his teeth on edge. He was so damn dependent his heart pounded as his feet quickened as he drew closer to home every night. His appetite for April was out of control. Most evenings he couldn't wait to touch her, to take her to bed. Instead of wanting her less as time went on, he wanted her more.

Yesterday he'd even blown off a meeting to come home at lunchtime to spend time with her. Her absence had filled him with a mixture of relief and annoyance. Relief that she wouldn't be aware of just how obsessive he'd become, and sexual frustration that she wasn't there.

In the bedroom Matthew stripped off his suit. He tossed his shirt into the empty hamper. She was so damned efficient. Doing his laundry, keeping his house clean. Preparing delicious meals every night.

With a curse he grabbed jeans from the wardrobe.

"You're in a crap mood." She stood in the doorway, watching him.

"I'm hungry."

She sat on the bed and pulled off her thick socks. "Let's go out then." She slipped her feet into shoes, and grabbed her bag from the floor.

She'd expressed a hankering for pizza, so they hadn't travelled far, just walked up to the pizzeria at the corner. Now, as he waited for the waitress to bring their meals, Matthew regretted the choice. The tiny restaurant was filled with people.

April swallowed a mouthful of red wine. "I heard from Elizabeth today."

Elizabeth? He searched in his memory, but came up empty.

"You remember Elizabeth? My landlady and boss?" Her head was tilted to the side, and the space between her eyebrows creased with a frown. They'd barely exchanged a word since he got home, so she was justified in feeling annoyed.

"Oh yeah, Elizabeth."

Their pizzas were put down on the table with a flourish by the waiter. When April smiled at him, he smiled back.

"Anyway…" She picked up a piece of pizza and chewed off a hunk. "They've finished the repair of the coffee shop and offered me my job back."

Whatever he'd been expecting, it hadn't been that.

April looked down at her plate. "The apartment has been refurbished too. She asked me if I wanted to move back in." The fingers of her right hand curled into her palm. Silence hung in the air for long moments. She was waiting for something. Something from him.

Do I want her to move out?

Before he had time to process the thought, April started talking, rapid-fire.

"I told her I would. And I'm going to have to give you notice on the job too."

"Give me notice? Is that all I am to you, a job?"

Her gaze pinned his. "You know damn well you're more to me, Matthew. But living with you was only ever going to be a part-time thing, wasn't it?"

"Things changed, though. Didn't they?" He didn't know why he felt so angry, but the urge to punch something made his muscles tense. "We started something."

"Yes." She crossed her arms, meal forgotten. "But me living in your house, dependent on you for everything isn't real life for either of us. We didn't make the decision to live together like this. It just happened." A muscle twitched in the corner of her jaw.

"Are you saying you don't want to be with me anymore?" Jeez, he sounded pathetic. And why exactly he was questioning her decision when earlier he'd had exactly the same thought, he didn't know. The thought of coming home to a house without her in it made his stomach clench, but at the same time, he wasn't ready to commit.

Maybe he'd never feel ready.

"Do you want me to stay? To make this permanent?"

There was no point in lying. "No."

April pulled in a shaky breath, and reached for her wineglass with trembling fingers. "I'll move out at the weekend." She drank deeply.

This wasn't ending. This couldn't be the end. Matthew covered her hand with his. "I don't want this to be over. We just need to slow things down a little. I'm just not ready…"

Her clear blue eyes shone with a trace of what might be unshed tears. "I'm not ready either." She pulled her hand away.

The food tasted like cardboard. When April's cell phone rang it was a welcome distraction from the tension simmering in the air between them. She fished it out of her bag and glanced at the display. "Hi, Dad."

Matthew rubbed the back of his neck. Irritated she still hadn't confessed to her family they were together.

"No, I'm just out having dinner with a friend." She shot him a glance.

The man on the other end of the phone was doing all the talking. She responded with terse yes and no's for a while. Then finished with, "I'll call you tomorrow and organize everything."

"June and Dad are in London. She wants to see the dress tomorrow. I'll take it to her hotel for the final fitting."

"You can invite them to the house."

She shook her head. "There's no need."

She didn't want to let her family know about him. Didn't want to rock the damn boat. "I'm not ashamed of our relationship with you, April. Are you?"

"The wedding is in two weeks. I don't see the point of introducing drama at this point."

Her words were so cool, someone who didn't know as well as he did might think she didn't care, but her body couldn't lie. The vein pulsed in her jaw; her fingers were curled into fists again.

"I'm not drama. I'm your man."

Her eyes softened. "Are you?"

*****

He'd kissed her outside the restaurant, his lips soundlessly telling her what he wouldn't say. They'd walked back to the house holding hands in silence, and when they got there had walked upstairs in the dark and made frantic love for hours.

She woke alone.

She'd pushed Matthew for a commitment and he'd pulled back, just as she knew he would. Her insides ached. The last meaningful thing he'd said was that he was her man, and yet he was prepared to let her move out, risk her walking away for good.

Tonight she'd be out for dinner with June and their father, and tomorrow she would move back into her apartment. She'd hired a van to transport her meager belongings, and co-opted Marie and Eliza in to help. They were full of questions she didn't want to answer but she'd promised full disclosure once she was safely back in her old apartment.

It was too painful to talk about before then.

Now, the thought of dragging June's dress across town to her hotel was beyond exhausting. Matthew's words from the previous night echoed in her mind. She wasn't ashamed of her relationship. And it wasn't over; it had merely shifted down a gear.

If there was to be any hope for a future with Matthew, she needed to obliterate some of the barriers. Up until now, cowardice had made her choose the easy option—the option of hiding her relationship with Matthew from her family, because avoidance felt a hell of a lot safer.

It was time to burst the bubble they'd been living in.

She could play it safe, or shake it up.

She picked up the phone.

June didn't answer her cell, so she left a message.

"June, instead of meeting at your hotel, grab a taxi this afternoon and come to me instead." She rattled off the address. *Let the fireworks begin.*

She'd told Matthew last night she was meeting June at the hotel. Now, she called him.

"Hi." His deep voice melted her insides, as usual.

"I've changed the arrangement with June. She's coming over."

Silence stretched for a long moment.

"Did you tell her about us?"

"Not yet." April glanced at her watch. "But she'll be here in a couple of hours. I just wanted to give you a heads up, in case you want to work late or something."

"I don't see any reason to avoid her. I told you last night,

I'm not ashamed we're together."

The warmth in his voice soothed her. "Okay, I'll see you later."

Being with Matthew wasn't easy. Her father would go ballistic, and the thought of yet another daughter being involved with Matthew Logan might cause her mother to have a heart attack. Mum's hatred of the man who'd run out on her eldest daughter was wrong, considering the facts, but she didn't know the facts, did she?

When June arrived two hours later, it was evident from her face that she got it. She knew exactly whose house April was living in. She stood on the doorstep in her Laboutin shoes and black skinny-jeans, with her long blonde hair falling in waves to the top of her breasts.

"Hi." She looked behind April, as if searching for someone else.

"Come in." April stepped back to let her sister in.

June kissed the air next to April's cheek. "So this is where you've been hiding!" With every step into Matthew's house her gaze took an inventory of his pictures, his furniture, his evident wealth. "Staying with a friend?"

April led her into the kitchen, unable to contemplate talking to her sister in the room where she and Matthew had first made love.

"I think you know exactly whose house this is."

June sat. "I sent an invitation to this house, so damn right I know whose house this is." Her eyes flashed and her nostrils flared a little. "What are you playing at, April?"

"I could ask you the same question." April pulled out a chair opposite. She sat and clasped her hands together on the table top. "I'm staying here with Matthew."

"I thought you didn't know where Matthew lived? As I

remember it, you didn't even know he lived in London."

"I didn't until you told me you'd invited him to the wedding. Then I looked up his address in the phone book and came out here to talk to him."

June's eyebrows rose in perfect arcs. "I don't see why."

"I came to ask Matthew not to come to your wedding. I thought it would be disruptive having the man who ran out on your previous wedding attend your current one."

June's face relaxed. "I told you why I invited him. I want people to forgive him. By inviting him to the wedding I was sending a message to everyone that I accept the choice he made, that I'm happy, and want him to be happy too."

"You want Matthew to be happy?" *Here it comes.*

"Of course."

"Happy with me?"

June frowned, as if not believing what she was hearing. "With you?" Her voice was so high it was almost a squeak.

April nodded. "With me."

"As in…a couple?" June had gone pale. Her gel nails fluttered, like painted bugs trying to fly away.

"Matthew and I are in a relationship."

"Oh, darling." June reached out and grabbed April's hand. Her head shook from side to side, setting her cloud of blonde hair bobbing. "Matthew isn't…Matthew doesn't…"

"Matthew doesn't what?"

June sighed. "Matthew has never got over me. This relationship with you, it's a way of getting back at me."

Wow, June's ego knows no limits.

"Matthew ran out on you years ago." *Tell me. Explain to me.*

June's gaze skittered to the corner of the room. Her

126

hand withdrew. "Ah, well..." She gazed into April's eyes, as if weighing up what April knew, and what she didn't. "It wasn't quite as clear-cut as that."

April breathed in, but said nothing.

"After the miscarriage we both decided it was a good idea not to go through with the wedding."

"You said it was his idea."

June bit her lip. "Well, we decided it would sound better if he was the one who didn't want—"

"What about the other men, June? The multiple possible fathers?"

June crossed her arms. "He told you?"

"He told me."

June pushed her hair back with a shaking hand. "I couldn't let Mum and Dad know about..." She swallowed. "I was young, boys chased me..."

"So you cheated on your boyfriend with other guys. Slept around and became pregnant. Why Matthew? Why did you choose him as the one you would marry?" She couldn't keep the anger in any longer, couldn't pretend to understand or to sympathize. June had destroyed her relationship with Matthew, with Amy. Had made him the bad guy and a pariah in Brookbridge. For what? Just to save her wretched reputation?

"Matthew was my boyfriend, the others were just..."

"Friends with benefits? Fuck-buddies? What?"

April stood and paced the floor.

"I was young." June whined.

"You were young seven years ago. You're not young now. Now, you're a grown woman still playing the sympathy card for being abandoned by the runaway groom. You could have told the truth any time over the last seven years, people would understand. But instead…" The blaze of anger was burning itself out, replaced by a simmering sadness. "People have hated him for deserting you. It isn't fair."

"Do you love him?"

None of your damn business. "That's between Matthew and me."

"Mum and Dad won't be happy about Matthew being in your life. I'm not happy about it."

April gritted her teeth together. "I don't think your opinion of my relationship is something I'm inclined to take into consideration."

"He's using you." June stood. "Face it, April. I sent him the invitation to my wedding, you turned up on the doorstep soon after, and he saw the perfect way to get back at me for loving someone else." She picked her bag off the table. "I'm going to have to see him, to talk to him about this. I don't want my little sister hurt."

In two steps April was toe-to-toe with her elegant sister. "Back off," she hissed. "Back off now, June." Her arms quivered with the strain of holding them at her sides.

"You don't understand anything about men." There was a bitter edge to June's words. Her mouth twisted. "There's no way any man is going to turn down a sure thing. And if you're living in his house, you're here, you're available."

"Stop." Bitter bile rose in April's throat.

"He's made you love him, hasn't he? I can't forgive him for that. And neither with Dad. We were going to take you out to dinner tonight."

"Did you come by taxi?" April walked to the kitchen door.

"No, I hired a car. It's parked outside."

"In that case, I suggest I give you your dress and you

can try it on at the hotel." She couldn't stand being in the same house as June for a moment longer, and she wouldn't be the one to leave. "If there are any problems with the fit you can tell me over dinner."

She took the stairs two at a time, slid the silver wedding gown into a dress cover and carried it downstairs.

"And if you could hold off from telling Dad about my relationship with Matthew, I'd appreciate it. I'll tell him myself."

She opened the front door wide, and watched her sister walk away.

Chapter Eleven

When Matthew got home, the familiar sound of the sewing machine hummed through the air. Clutching the box he'd brought from work, he climbed the stairs. June must still be here. He didn't want to see her. Any love he'd ever had for her had seeped away months after their split. In retrospect he'd been in love with someone who didn't really exist.

She'd always courted attention, even back in school. Had needed to be the most popular, the one receiving the most attention.

April and June were as different as chalk and cheese. April always sought to fade into the background, dressing in black and wearing the bare minimum of make-up. Instead of artifice, her true self shone. She was funny and charming. Sexy and sweet. She'd effortlessly charmed not only him but everyone in his office. She'd even charmed his clients. The gift he clutched in his hands demonstrated that more clearly than anything.

Letting June visit her here meant she'd decided to go public with their relationship, no matter what her sister had to say about it. Matthew had left the office as soon as possible to be here and support her.

He pushed the door open. The machine's noise drifted to quiet.

April turned. Her smile made something twist inside. "No June?"

"She's been and gone." She took the strip of material from the machine and walked over.

"Is it bad of me to say I'm glad I missed her?"

She linked her arms around his waist and smiled up into his face. "I wish I'd missed her."

Matthew smoothed a hand over her chestnut hair. "Was it bad?"

She nodded. "Battle of the Titans bad. I threw her out."

He felt his eyes widen. Leaned down and kissed her, because he couldn't resist. Her lips parted and his tongue slipped inside, tangling with hers. His body reacted as it always did with the taste of April, springing into instant life.

His hands slid over her curves.

"Hey." She pulled back. "I have to get ready to go out. Why don't you come talk to me while I dress?"

"I love watching you get dressed. Especially if it involves you taking clothes off before putting other clothes on." He waggled his eyebrows, and felt joy explode inside as she laughed.

"You, Matthew Logan, are a complete perv."

"That's why you love me."

She glanced away. "That must be it."

The words had slipped out without thought. They'd never spoken of love. Never let those words pass either of their lips during any of the hot night-time encounters.

She stepped away, and picked the piece of fabric she'd been working on from the table. "What do you think?" She held it up for his perusal. A wide swatch of emerald fabric, studded with black beads in an intricate pattern.

"It's gorgeous. What is it?"

"It's a belt," she explained as if talking to an infant. "I had this piece in my remnants box, and it was so beautiful, I thought I'd dress up my long black dress a bit." She wrapped it around her narrow waist on top of her jeans, and fastened it in the back. "You like?" She noticed the box he was holding in one hand. "What's that?"

He took her hand. "I'll show you while you get dressed."

He sat on the bed while she rooted around in the wardrobe.

"So, what's in the box?" She glanced over her shoulder.

"It's a present that arrived in my office today. From Albios. To you."

"To me?" She strode over, sat, and picked up the box. She ripped off the brown paper to reveal a shoebox. Inside was a pair of black Albios running shoes and a thick plastic envelope. "Wow." She searched inside. "They got my size right and everything."

"She rang me to check."

One eyebrow rose. "And you didn't tell me?"

"I thought you liked surprises."

"I do." She pulled out the thick envelope and ripped it open. A black top and matching running shorts fell out when she tipped the packet on the bed. Both had hot pink stripes down the side. There was a card, which she read aloud. "April, we thought you'd like these. Matthew said you hadn't entered the women's 10k at the end of the month, but we've registered a place for you in case you'd like to. Best, Angela."

She held up the short top—barely more than a sports

bra. "That's so nice of her."

"Might you run the 10k?"

She grimaced. "I think my experience at the race-track proves pretty definitively I'm not in good shape for running."

"You didn't prepare though, did you? How long had it been since you'd done any running?"

"Years," she confessed. "I didn't expect it to be so intense."

"We could run every evening. I haven't been out for the past couple of weeks, and I could do with the exercise." Leaning close he watched her eyes darken. "I could train you."

"You wouldn't consider stuffing a bra and joining in disguise, then? Because if you did I'd definitely enter."

Even the thought made him shudder. "No way. No way in hell."

She stripped off her jeans and pulled her shirt over her head.

Matthew's synapses misfired. *What were we talking about?* He stepped close and ran his hand over her flat stomach. "You have a runner's physique."

She picked his hand off, like a diligent gardener picking a caterpillar from a rose. "Much as I love you touching me, I'm running against the clock here." She pressed her lips to his. "And I'm going to be late back tonight, so don't wait up." She picked up the long black dress and stepped into it.

"I'll be awake."

She fastened the wide emerald belt around her waist.

"What happened with June?"

"She basically told me the only reason you and I are together is because you're getting back at her for marrying someone else." Her full lips compressed into a tight line. "She only admitted the truth about the wedding when I confronted her."

"You know that's bullshit, right?" What he had felt for June couldn't compare with the feelings he had for April. Anger rose in a wave he hadn't been there to put June straight. "Can I come with you to dinner? I'd like to make sure they both understand how I feel about you."

"I don't even understand how you feel about me."

"I care about you. You turn me inside out, and every time I'm with you, I want to drag you into bed."

"That's not caring, Matthew. That's lust." Her smile held no trace of anger. "I know all about lust." Her eyes flicked down his body and up again.

"It's more than lust. A lot more than lust." He grabbed her hand and kissed her palm. "You're the only woman I want."

She blinked. The smile faded and confusion clouded her eyes. "I'm getting a lot of mixed signals here."

She was right. One minute he was encouraging her to move out, and the next declaring how she was the only woman he wanted. The two positions were un-reconcilable polar opposites.

"I know." He ran a hand across her cheekbones. He couldn't explain, couldn't offer any more insight into the workings of his mind. Logic told him to pull back, but other more powerful emotions demanded he did the very opposite. "I guess I'm confused."

"Join the club." Her voice was low and husky. "But I know one thing. You're in my life and it's about time every member of my family knows it." She straightened. "So thanks for the offer of joining us for dinner, but I'll handle it alone."

*****

What she needed now was distance. Distance from the emotions that rose in her every time she was in the same room with Matthew. Over the past weeks she'd become so used to their life together the prospect of not seeing him automatically every night made her melancholy. In one way, June had been right. Living with him, there was no choice involved about whether they would be together or not—their overwhelming physical attraction overrode everything. He said it was more than lust, but had baulked at the thought of more.

Distance.

A few drops of rain splattered on the ground as she dashed from taxi to her father's hotel.

He was waiting in the foyer.

"Hi, honey."

She breathed in her father's familiar scent as he hugged her tight. It had been too long since she'd seen him, and being in his arms made her feel safe, as it always had.

"Hi, Dad." She glanced around. "No June?"

"She's checking out the room service menu." He didn't look happy. Obviously June had revealed what had gone down during the afternoon. "Let's go through and order, I'm starving."

His five-star hotel had a Michelin starred restaurant and as such was packed.

Jack gave his name to the hostess, who led them to a reserved table in a quiet corner. The waitress handed over menus and left them to consider.

"You and June had a fight, I hear." He didn't look up from the wine list.

"We did. Did she tell you what about?"

His gaze flicked up. "Yes. But I'd like to hear your side of the story."

The waitress interrupted and they both quickly ordered.

"I'm staying with Matthew Logan. He and I…"

Her father's gaze was steady. He waited for her to continue.

April swallowed. "He and I are in the early stages of a relationship." A relationship that could be ended tomorrow, for all she knew.

Jack's lips compressed. "June told me she thought he'd become involved with you to get back at her for her wedding."

April's mouth opened.

Jack held up a hand. "Before you start— I don't believe that for a moment. June and Matthew were over years ago, and I see no reason to believe he wouldn't be captivated by you just for yourself. June has a robust ego."

"Did she tell you anything else?" April bet she didn't. June wouldn't want to give up her victimized bride tag to easily.

"What else is there? You're not…" Jack paled, as if the past had risen from the dead.

"I'm not getting married, and I'm not pregnant. June misrepresented what went on back then, Dad. She admitted as much when I confronted her."

Jack's rare steak arrived, and the waitress put down a plate of ravioli before April.

The moment they were alone again, Jack sighed. "Let's have it then."

Part of April felt bad, ratting out her sister. But the other part, the other part wanted desperately for her father to understand, to stop blaming Matthew for the events that had happened so many years ago. He deserved to have his side of the story heard, especially as it was the truth.

"When June lost the baby, Matthew was prepared to continue with the wedding, but June wasn't." She sucked in a breath. "June was sleeping with someone else at the same time as she was sleeping with Matthew..."

Her father swore, and his knife clattered on the plate. Their eyes met.

"She confirmed it to me today, Dad."

With a curt nod, he gestured she should continue.

"She told him she wasn't sure the baby was his, and said now they didn't have to get married, she didn't want to be tied down. She thought she was too young."

"Why the hell didn't she just tell me?"

"She didn't want you to think badly of her. She asked Matthew to be the bad guy, to be the one who called off the wedding, so you, me and Mum wouldn't think..."

"She had loose morals." Her father sawed at his steak as though it was made of wood.

"Yes."

He shook his head and swallowed a mouthful of wine. "When she settled on Matthew your mother and I were relieved. She'd always been flighty, and he seemed such a solid young man." His mouth twisted. "I'd forgive both of you girls anything, you know that, right?"

He leaned in, a desperate look in his eyes. "We would have worked it out. It would have been a blow, but we'd have forgiven her. She was young, and people make mistakes when they're young."

He rubbed his forehead with both hands. "She's not young any more. And the fact she's let us think badly of

Matthew for so many years is…" He looked so appalled, April's heart twisted. "It's a terrible thing to do."

"I'm sure she just didn't want to disappoint you, Dad." The words were intended as a balm to her father's shattered feelings, not an excuse for her sister's behavior.

"I'm sure she wanted to bask in everyone's sympathy." His eyes dimmed. "Unfortunately I'm probably to blame for this as much as everyone. I've always spoilt her."

The food was delicious, but April had no appetite.

"He's a brave man, getting involved with our family again. I should meet him, tell him I'm sorry."

"You have nothing to be sorry for. You were acting on shaky information, but you were sticking up for June." April covered her father's hand on the white linen tablecloth. "Matthew understands."

"I hope to meet him again sometime soon. Perhaps I can visit…"

"Matthew gave me somewhere to stay while my apartment was being renovated. I'm moving out this weekend."

"I thought you and he…"

"We're taking it slow. Moving in with him was only ever going to be a temporary arrangement."

"Are you happy, peanut?" The childhood nickname warmed her.

"I'm happy." She could be happier, and maybe she would be, once she got back to her life and untangled her emotions some. But right now, she was happy everyone knew the truth, and her father had enough sensitivity to accept her sister's flaws without disowning her.

Matthew was asleep on the sofa in front of a flickering TV when she got home. As promised, he'd waited up. She stood in the doorway, fighting back the urge to wake him. With the prospect of moving out so near, their lovemaking would be bittersweet.

She turned away. Tomorrow was Friday, their final day living together.

Her hands clenched into fists. If tonight was bad, tomorrow would be even worse. She couldn't face it. It would be easier to move tomorrow, while he was out at work rather prolonging the agony.

*****

When Matthew woke in the morning, he rubbed his hands over his eyes and immediately worried April hadn't made it back last night. He climbed upstairs, and checked out his bedroom. Empty.

Without expectation, he turned the doorknob of the spare room.

April lay spread-eagled in the large bed, her chestnut hair fanned out on the pillow. Matthew stepped back quietly so as not to wake her, and pulled the door closed behind him.

For some reason she'd decided not to wake him on her return the previous night. He ran through the possible reasons as he stood under the shower, letting the pounding spray soothe his aching muscles.

By the time he made it into the office, he had a plan in place.

He'd make tonight a night to remember. Maybe another dinner-cruise on the Thames? They hadn't danced last time, and the thought of holding her while floating past London's landmarks felt right.

Nothing feels right about April moving out.

He rubbed his head. How had April become so vital to

his existence in such a short time? He couldn't backtrack now, not when the reasons for distance were so clearly valid. He didn't want a full-time, serious relationship. The thought of handing her his heart brought him out in a sweat.

Dinner, dancing, distance. He picked up the phone, and called the dinner cruise company.

Chapter Twelve

April moved out while Matthew was at work.

Eliza had a full-day meeting, so couldn't make it, but Marie readily agreed to come help April move, and what's more, added her unemployed brother's brawn into the mix.

By mid-afternoon, she and all of her possessions were back in her repainted apartment, so she settled down on the sofa and called Matthew.

"Hi." He sounded distracted. "What's going on?"

"I decided to move a day earlier."

He didn't respond.

"I thought it would be easier."

"Easier how?"

Easier on me. "I didn't see the point of putting it off for another day. Marie and her brother were available, and I was able to get the van, so I've moved." She forced a brightness she didn't feel into her voice. "The girls are coming over later for dinner."

"Fine." His voice was flat. "Maybe I'll see you over the weekend."

"I'll probably be working. The coffee shop is re-opening on Saturday." She crossed her fingers. She wasn't scheduled to work until Monday, but she needed time away from Matthew to regain her equilibrium. "How about I call you next week?"

"I may have to go out of the country next week." He didn't elaborate, and she didn't ask. "I'll call you when I'm back."

April closed her eyes. Things unsaid hung in the air between them. She wanted to tell him how she missed him already. How it felt as though her heart was breaking. How she wanted nothing more than to invite him over and spend the weekend in bed with him.

Those words couldn't be said, yet keeping them inside made her heart ache. She yearned for him. What had begun as a casual affair had become so much more. Now, she was caught in a maelstrom of dangerous currents, dragging her down into a love that wasn't reciprocated. Instead of drowning in them, she needed to reach for the lifebelt of distance, and save herself.

She rubbed her thumb over the thimble.

"Take care, Matthew." She hung up.

*****

He'd got what he wanted, a breathing space, so why did he feel so goddamned angry?

Matthew stood up and stalked around his desk, mind racing. He tracked across the carpet, turned, then strode back. After the call from Albios, he should be jubilant, should be making arrangements. Instead, shock thundered through him that April had already moved out.

And disappointment the night he'd planned wouldn't happen crushed any hope of celebrating.

It took three tracks of the shag-pile carpet before he realized he was pacing, something he always did when he was agitated. He didn't even know how the dinner with her father and June had gone last night.

He pulled in a deep breath then let it out slowly. She'd blown him off, and he had no one to blame but himself. There was no point in even thinking about it anymore, he had other more pressing things demanding his attention.

He dialed Jason's extension. "We need to talk."

"Problem?"

"No."

"I'll be right there."

In moments Jason pushed Matthew's office door open, stepped in, and sat. "So, what's happening?"

"I just got a call from Angela at Albios. The American branch is very interested in the system, and she's asked if I could do a presentation to them in New York."

Jason's eyebrows rose. "Wow. That's huge."

Matthew nodded. "They are sponsoring a lot of marathons and mini-marathons over the next year, and want to see a demonstration before committing themselves, but yes, it could be a lot of business for us." He straightened the papers on his desk. "They want to see me next week. I'll need you to tweak the previous presentation and organize a similar set-up as we had at the airfield."

"In New York somewhere?" Jason frowned. He tapped his fingertips on his thigh. Then he nodded. "I have someone I can call." He stood. "I'll get right on it."

"Send Susan in on your way out, will you? I need her to book my flights."

"Will do, Boss."

A change of scene would do him good, and rather than stay in a hotel and brood, he'd call his brother Adam and beg a bed. Jason could handle things in the office, so maybe he'd even stay for a few extra days.

He was normally stoked at being in a new place. Adam's apartment overlooking Central Park was spacious and modernistic, with a place for everything and everything in its place. Unfortunately, even his brother's obsessive tidiness made Matthew think of April.

Adam was a bit of a recluse, but he'd made an effort to line up things for them to do. The first day and night Matthew had been busy with Albios, but yesterday they'd signed the contract and tonight, by rights, he should be celebrating.

The person he wanted to share his success with wasn't there. And he'd made a stupid decision to not call her while he was away—in a misguided attempt to prove to himself he didn't have to share every last detail of his life with her.

As a result he was bloody miserable.

"So. What do you want to do tonight?" Adam pushed his tortoiseshell glasses up with a long finger. "I have a couple of girls who would be on for dinner," he grimaced. "Or we could catch a game or something?"

Adam had never been into sports, he spent most of his time pounding his computer keys. The guy practically lived online.

"What would you be doing tonight if I weren't here?"

Adam pushed a hand through his hair, making it stand straight up. His gaze skittered to the side of the room, and he looked decidedly uncomfortable. "Uh…"

There was something here, something he wasn't telling. Matthew pushed. "Come on, out with it."

Adam's embarrassment was evident. He walked over to the mantle, and picked up two tickets propped there. "I have tickets to Stacy's show."

"Tonight?"

"Yeah." Adam looked down at his feet. "She's only playing one night in New York."

"Does she know…"

Adam's gaze flicked up, eyes wide and shocked. "Christ no. The only reason I got the tickets was because it's a huge show, there's no way she'd spot me in the audience."

His entire family had been amazed when his geeky brother had managed to snare the attention of country music star Stacy Gold. When their Vegas marriage had ended in divorce three months later, no one was surprised. It was astounding to learn that a year later Adam still carried a torch though.

Curiosity spiked. "What happened with you two?"

Adam shrugged. "Oh, you know, stuff. I don't understand women."

"Me neither." A dark cloud filled Matthew's chest. He didn't understand what women wanted, hell, he didn't understand what he wanted.

"You having women trouble, bro?" Adam walked to the fridge, pulled out a couple of beers and handed one over. "I thought you were smooth with the ladies."

"Once upon a time." Until he'd let April get under his skin. "I'm in way over my head."

"Who with?"

Being on the other end of an interrogation wasn't fun. Matthew slugged a mouthful of beer. "Do you remember April Leigh?"

Adam's eyebrows shot up. "Little April? June's sister?"

"That's the one." No longer little April, but all grown-up April. The woman he couldn't stop thinking about, the woman he wanted to be with, even if being with her meant he was in danger of getting his heart broken again.

Adam shook his head. "You look like you've got it bad."

"Takes one to know one."

The corner of Adam's mouth twitched. "Yeah, we're pathetic."

Matthew strolled over and picked the tickets out of Adam's hand. "So, what time does this concert start?"

Chapter Thirteen

Absence makes the heart grow fonder.

Evicted from her bedroom in favor of an elderly aunt, April lay on the fold-down sofa in the sitting-room of her mother's house.

The stupid saying was true. The past six days had proved it without a doubt. She'd moved out, but she might as well have fallen off the edge of the earth. Her mobile rang, but the caller was never Matthew. More than once, she considered calling, but had instead called Maria or Eliza instead. They never held the fact she was a mental wreck against her.

He'd said he would be away for the week. Presumably in the far reaches of the Amazon rainforest, or on the top of a mountain peak—some remote place on the planet without cell-phone coverage. Or memories.

Being back at work had been a godsend, because it kept her busy. Joshua kept inviting her out, between creating his trademark coffee-leaf swirls atop cappuccinos. Maybe she should take him up on his offer, anything would be better than endless angsting over Matthew. Maybe when she got back from the wedding she'd say yes.

The flight to Dublin had been quick, and her mother had insisted on picking her up from the airport. Every room in the house was filled with relatives, it was impossible to find any quiet corner to sit and brood.

After the initial awkwardness, she'd made peace with June, whose excitement was palpable. The day after tomorrow the all-consuming family wedding would at last be over. The relatives would move out, and she and her mother would be alone for a couple of days before it was time to return to London.

Her cell phone rang in the darkness.

"I miss you." Matthew's voice was deep and urgent.

April held the phone from her ear and looked at the time. "You called me at quarter to one in the morning to tell me you miss me?"

"I didn't think of the time. It's earlier here. I'm staying with my brother."

"Where are you?"

"New York. I don't want to talk about that, I just had to tell you I was thinking about you." The words were almost growled, as though he resented the compulsion. "I think of you all the damn time. It's driving me crazy."

Joy burst inside April. At least she wasn't the only one suffering this affliction.

"So, if it's the middle of the night, you're in bed?" His voice deepened.

"I'm not in *my* bed." Six long days and nights without a word. He probably hadn't even registered June's wedding was tomorrow.

"Are you alone?" The sharpness in his tone was evidence he didn't like the idea of her being in someone else's bed one bit.

"I'm alone," she admitted. "And I'm not even in a bed at all. I'm squashed on a lumpy sofa in my mother's house. The wedding is the day after tomorrow, remember?"

"Damn, I'd forgotten. I'm back in London tomorrow. I'd planned on taking a taxi straight to your apartment."

"For?"

"For you. These past days without you have been torture. How long before you come home?"

"I'm staying with Mum for a couple of days after the wedding." The thought of cutting her visit short was tempting, but she doused it with a bucket of cold logic. She stroked her stomach under the duvet. "So, you've missed me."

"You haven't told me you missed me too."

"I have. I do." She felt the muscles of her stomach contract under fingers. Lying here in the darkness with his sexy voice in her ear was enough to imagine he was lying with her. On her. "I'm lying here in the dark missing you." His swift indrawn breath gave her courage. "Imagining your hands on me."

"I..." He cleared his throat. "What are you wearing?"

A tatty oversized tee-shirt didn't sound very appealing, so she improvised. "A short red satin nightgown."

"Anything under it?"

"Not a thing. You?"

"I'm taking my clothes off and climbing into bed."

April's heart thudded.

"I'm imagining you lying next to me. Can you feel my hand pushing down the straps of your nightgown?"

Her mouth dried. "Yes." Her body went lax, her legs opening. "Your mouth is on my neck."

"My hands are cupping your breasts. You know how

much I love your breasts, don't you?"

"Bite me."

Matthew groaned.

The fact that everyone else in the house was upstairs asleep, and she couldn't be overheard gave April courage to take things further.

"I'm touching you." Her voice was husky. "Stroking your chest, your abs."

"Go lower."

"You're so hard for me."

"I'm always hard thinking of you, being with you. Take the nightgown off."

April pulled the tee-shirt over her head and threw it on the floor. "I'm naked."

"Touch yourself," he muttered. "Feel me brushing against your clit."

Her fingers rubbed against her sensitive nub. Her nipples were so hard they ached.

"You're so beautiful. Your nipple is in my mouth, I can't get enough of your taste."

Matthew's words were almost enough. Almost. "My hand is around you, stroking down then up again. I love the feel of you against me. I'm so wet, so ready." She bit her bottom lip—tasted blood. She moaned, knowing exactly what the sound would do to him. "You're sliding into me. Filling me."

"You're gripping me so tight. Feel me move inside you."

"Oh, Matthew."

"April." His voice was a dark whisper in her ear. "April… Come with me. Come for me."

Her breaths were little more than gasps as her fingers brought her close to the edge. The sound of Matthew's muttered endearments as she surrendered to sensation was more erotic than she would have believed possible. When the shudders engulfed her entire body she whispered his name and heard him reach orgasm a moment later.

April pulled the covers up and wrapped her arms around herself as her heart-rate steadied.

"That was incredible, but it wasn't enough. I need more than a dream of you," Matthew said. "Call me with your flight details and I'll pick you up at the airport."

"I'm getting in on Monday morning. You'll be in work."

"Wrong." He made a sound somewhere between a laugh and a groan. "I'll be waiting at the arrivals gate for you. I might even camp out at the airport for the next few days—without you there's nothing to come home to."

"You could climb on a flight to Dublin." The words were out before her mind caught up, but the idea was attractive. After tonight, the thought of three more days without him was tortuous. "I won't be able to get away to pick you up, but…"

"How did dinner with your father and June go?"

"June bailed. It was just the two of us." She pulled in a breath. "Even after the conversation with me, June hadn't told Dad, so I did. He's sorry about the way he treated you, he wants to meet and make amends."

Matthew was silent for a long moment. "Then there's nothing to stop me coming to the wedding, as your date."

April's heart thudded. Appearing at the wedding, making it clear to her family and all Brookbridge he was with her was close to a declaration of love. "Are you sure?"

"Yes." His voice was definite. "I'll get a taxi from the airport, and see you in the church, if not before."

*****

There were some times in life April wished the ground would just open and she could fall in. This was one of those times.

June was wearing heels so high she'd break her ankle if she fell over. Her skirt just about covered her bottom. She looked ridiculous.

And she'd provided neon mini-dresses to make sure every single one of the six female friends she was dragging out tonight for her pre-wedding party was dressed ridiculously too. Including April.

"I'm not feeling so great, maybe I'll just…"

June held out a hand palm out. "Hold it right there." She scowled. "There's no way in hell you're escaping my hen night, get used to it. I'm going to need someone to stay sober and make sure I get back tonight, and as my sister that duty falls to you."

She balanced the pink sequined cowboy hat over her blonde waves, and fastened the 'bride-in-waiting' sash across her chest. "Tonight will be fun! Drinking, dancing," her eyebrows rose suggestively, "men."

"Men?" Sheesh, just when she wanted to sound nonchalant, she was squeaking like a mouse. "As in more than one?"

"I certainly hope so." June smoothed over the tiny pleated skirt skimming her derriere.

April swiped a hand across her clammy forehead. "It's just…the wedding is tomorrow, you should take it easy and make sure you're not hung over."

"This is my last night of freedom. I intend to have fun." June took a tiny compact from her bag and examined her reflection. "You could do with a little fun too. Or are you afraid Matthew will object?"

They hadn't mentioned Matthew since the day at his house. "I'm my own person. I don't need Matthew's approval."

June picked at the edge of her gel nail, feinting nonchalance. "So it's still going on then, is it? The thing with Matthew? Only you haven't mentioned him, and I wondered if it had fizzled."

"I know he didn't reply to the invitation, so he won't be coming to the reception, but he's coming to the wedding."

June's eyes opened wide. "Seriously?"

"Seriously."

"What about all the reasons you stated for him not being there?"

"Dad will be fine with it…"

"And Mum?"

Mum. Their mother had never forgiven Matthew for the imagined sin of running out on June. The possibility that she would react badly, even that her heart might give out seeing Matthew at the church was a very real one. "I need to talk to her." April turned to the door.

"Talk to her tomorrow morning, before the wedding. The longer she has to think about it, the worse it will be." June tilted her head to the sitting-room. "Right now, she's having fun with her sisters. Do you really want to destroy tonight for her too?"

Gales of laughter floated in the air from the room next door. June was right. Mum was having more fun than she'd had all year, and bringing Matthew into the discussion right now would definitely damped the celebration. All of April's aunts were one hundred percent anti-Matthew too, so they'd all get involved.

She groaned.

"Anyway, you and I have somewhere to be tonight." June's gaze flicked the length of the neon minidress she'd provided as hen-night wear for all the bridesmaids. "Pull up those knee-socks and let's go out and see if the limo is here yet."

What happens to women when they go to a hen-night?

If the pack of rowdy revelers stuffed into the back of the limo was any indication, they turned into crazed nymphomaniacs. No doubt her abstinence colored her judgment. The others had been downing jelly shots like they were going out of style. She'd already had to prise a tall stranger's hands off her sister's backside in the second pub they'd crawled to. And then had June pout at her as though she was being an old stick-in-the-mud.

And they hadn't even got to the nightclub yet.

Bren swigged from an open bottle of champagne, rubbed her hand over the top, and handed it to June. "We'll have a couple of drinks in O'Brien's, then we're off to the club."

April knew she was frowning, but reckoned she was entitled. At this rate they wouldn't be home until the early hours, and the amount of drink June had consumed meant she'd doubtless be throwing up before morning.

If Mum and her sisters were still up when they got home, there'd be hell to pay. And June would be out of it, so the wrath of her elders would fall squarely on April.

The limo slowed and stopped outside the last pub on the pub-crawl, O'Brien's.

One by one, like drunken lemmings, the girls stumbled out.

April brought up the rear, picking up a discarded sparkly Stetson and carrying one of Bren's shoes abandoned in her rush to get inside.

The entire pub turned and gawked at their entrance.

Oh great.

"Kiss the bride!" Bren squawked to the room in general, waving at June. "It's her last night of freedom! Anything goes!"

A couple of guys looked interested and sauntered over, so April stalked in front of her sister like a miniature bodyguard. "They've had too much to drink, lads," she said quietly. "Back off, would you?"

With sympathetic grins, they returned to their seats.

"Ah, April," Bren wailed. "We're supposed to be having fun!" She scanned the bar then stopped and licked her lips. "OMG I think I see...." She started across the room, in a funny up and down gait as one foot was clad in a six inch heel, and the other bare. "I do!" Her hands flailed in the air as she reached her intended target. "Nick Logan. I thought it was you!" Without ceremony she plonked down on his knee.

Matthew's brother. The only one of his siblings who still lived in Brookbridge. June and the rest of the hens seemed safe enough attacking shots lined up on the bar, so April went to his rescue.

She held out Bren's shoe. "Hi, Nick."

Nick Logan was the town vet. He looked as though he regretted not bringing a tranquilizer gun with him. *I bet he doesn't get mauled like this on a daily basis.*

Bren put her shoe on, almost falling off Nick's knee in the process. When she straightened, she whacked him in the eye with her pink sequined cowboy hat.

Nick winced, and then mouthed "Help" at April.

"You're missing out on vodka shots, Bren."

Bren plastered a kiss square on Nick's startled face. "Gotta run, sweet thing. We're going on from here to Mulligans. Maybe you'll join us?"

"Uh, I've got a busy day tomorrow, so I doubt it."

Bren pouted. She stood on wobbly legs, and wandered away.

Nick's face was a picture of relief. "Thanks, April. So, big day tomorrow?"

"Yes. The wedding is at eleven." Once, she'd been totally relaxed with every member of the Logan family, but over the past few years she'd avoided them all. It felt good to break the ice.

Gales of feminine laughter reached her from across the room. "I'm charged with keeping this lot in check. I better go." Nick's smile reminded her of Matthew's. "It was good to see you."

He covered well, but she caught the flash of surprise in his eyes. "Good to see you too. I hope it all goes well tomorrow. Do give June my congratulations."

"I will." She patted Nick's shoulder, and went back to bridesmaid-wrangling.

The spirit was willing, but the flesh was weak—probably due to the fact that the spirits had been consumed by the flesh, and the result wasn't pretty.

Despite the desire to stay in the club until closing time, various members of the party were decidedly worse for wear, and it was becoming increasingly more difficult to look after all of them.

April called the limo and arranged a pick-up.

They'd dropped off the others at their homes, and now only June and April sat in the limo parked outside their house.

"Can you give us a couple of minutes, Tony?" June asked the driver.

He nodded, climbed out, and lit a cigarette.

June placed a hand over April's. "I just wanted to talk to you before we…" She waved a hand in the direction of the dark house. "Well, I just wanted to say I'm sorry." She stared at the limo's carpet. "I'm sorry I never told you the truth about Matthew."

"It doesn't matter."

June's gaze snapped to April's. "Yes. It does matter. I ruined your friendship with Amy, and when you told me you and he were together, I almost poisoned that too."

She looked so wretched, April's heart clenched. "I just don't understand why you couldn't tell me."

"I thought you'd hate me." June chewed her bottom lip. "You looked up to me, and the thought you'd lose respect for me, you wouldn't like me anymore…" Her eyes filled with tears. "I'm an awful person."

Alcohol always made June maudlin, but there was a core of truth to her words. "You're not an awful person." April hugged her sister close. "I guess I've been pretty judgmental in the past. I'm sorry too."

All her life she'd seen things in black and white, putting some people like her sister on pedestals, and damning others. It was hardly surprising June had wanted approval so much she'd been afraid to reveal the truth of her first wedding break-up.

Everyone deserved a second chance. And people she loved deserved more—they deserved her understanding for whatever choices they made.

April found a tissue in her bag and wiped the mascara trails from her sister's eyes. "I love you, June." She reached for the door handle. "Now, let's get you to bed."

*****

There wasn't a cloud in the sky the next morning.

With a team of aunties giving the bride breakfast-in-bed together with copious jugs of coffee, April slipped into her mother's bedroom. "I need to talk to you."

Margaret Leigh pulled her robe tighter and sat down on the bed. "Is everything okay, April?"

April nodded and sat down next to her mother. "I've been seeing someone and it's serious."

Margaret's face lit with a smile. *This next bit was going to be hard.*

"I want you to have an open mind." She warned heart sinking as her mother's expression changed to worry. She breathed in deep. "It's Matthew Logan."

Margaret's eyes widened. "Matthew."

"Yes. Matthew." She grasped her mother's hand. "I know you don't like him, I know you think…"

Margaret's mouth thinned. "He ran out on your sister."

"I've spoken to June, and it turns out he didn't. The end of their relationship was a joint decision. They were both very young, and if they'd married it's more than likely they'd have broken up by now. June and Michael are perfect together. They're having a perfect wedding today, one that will last. I care about Matthew."

Her mother's eyes took on a faraway look. "I always liked him. I was so disappointed when they broke up. I can't understand why June wouldn't just tell us their breaking up was a mutual thing."

"She didn't want us to be angry with her."

Margaret thought for a long moment. "All of the wedding preparations had gone ahead. I suppose it was easier on her to be the jilted one than calling it off." Her mouth tilted in a smile. "I can't believe you decided to wait until this morning to tell me."

"June invited Matthew to the wedding. And he's going to be there."

"Ah. Does your father know?"

"I told him the last time I saw him. He's okay with it."

Margaret stood. "Then I'm okay with it too." She pulled her daughter into a hug. "Now go and help your sister into her dress."

April floated to the door, as if a heavy weight had been lifted from her shoulders.

"April."

She turned at the doorway.

"If he hurts you, I'll kill him."

Chapter Fourteen

June had been transformed from a pale, hung over wreck to Helen of Troy. Or at least April's idea of what Helen of Troy should have looked like.

Her long blonde hair curled around her shoulders. The silver wedding dress fit perfectly and gleamed in the afternoon sun as she stepped from the wedding car and glided up the path to the old stone church.

What was most beautiful about her was the look on her face. Pure, unadulterated joy.

April sighed.

She hadn't heard from Matthew, and had no idea what time his flight was getting in, but with luck he'd be already in the church. Her heart quickened at the thought of seeing him again. Her mother had broken the news to all her relatives, and laid down the law. They were to shelve any lingering bad feelings they had about Matthew and treat him like a member of the family.

All of the obstacles to April's very own happy-ever-after were dissolving. June had even insisted the caterers add a place for him at the reception.

"Come on!" Bren hissed.

April scurried to join the rest of the bridal party as inside the church the organist started to play *Here comes the bride.*

In this church, her parents had wed. Her grandfather and grandmother too. The walls had seen generations of her family celebrate love, baptize their children, and when life ended, had celebrated their lives in their funeral services.

One day, maybe, Matthew and April would walk down this aisle together.

April mis-stepped as the thought took hold, but quickly recovered. Her gaze scanned the pews left and right.

The church was packed with friends and relatives, as well as a healthy contingent of the groom's family who had flown in from the States. By the time the small procession reached the altar, she hadn't spotted Matthew. Perhaps his flight had been delayed.

As the marriage service got underway, she glanced back over her shoulder at the entrance. She held her breath as the vicar asked if anyone objected to the wedding, breathed out in relief when the church was so silent for a moment you could hear the silk on June's dress rustle.

His flight must have been delayed.

Her phone was off, but when they came back out into the sunshine and she turned it back on, no doubt there'd be a voice message, or a text.

There wasn't.

Hope took a long time to die. It felt a bit unwell outside the church, needed oxygen all the way through the reception, and suffered a heart attack when April stepped sideways rather than catch her sister's tossed bouquet.

Not a word from Matthew.

Not one single, freaking word.

She was sick and tired of checking her phone. Sick and

tired of rebuffing enquiries about his absence from concerned relatives. But still hope lingered on life-support. The possibility still existed there was an explanation for his absence. Maybe there was a problem with the flight, maybe he'd missed it.

If so, why hadn't he rung?

She'd moved into June's room as the party continued into the night.

He should ring. Should text. She should wait it out.

She texted him. "Where are you?"

Long moments later, he texted back. "I'm sorry, April. I'm not coming."

Hope took its last breath and died.

*****

Matthew didn't want to have this conversation by text. He didn't want to call her either. What needed to be said needed to be face-to-face. Unfortunately the choice he'd made in the airport made that impossible.

He'd booked the flight to Dublin. Had arrived at the airport with plenty of time.

And at the last moment, had chickened out.

The suggestion to join her in Brookbridge had been his; she'd even asked if he were sure. There was no way he could blame her for this situation.

Waiting for the flight to be called, he'd thought about walking back into her family's life after so many years, so much history. Appearing at the wedding with April was a firm statement of intent. They'd joke how she and Matthew would be next. Would have the whole wedding planned before he'd even made the decision to ask her to marry him. The pressure of conforming to her family's expectations had brought him out in a cold sweat.

What was between them was between *them*, not the whole goddamned town.

He hadn't been able to stop thinking about her during the entire time he was in New York. He wanted her with an urgency without limits. But April had said it was just lust, had never said she wanted more. The jump between bed-partner and husband-to-be was too far for him to take.

So before they'd called his flight he'd stepped back to the desk and changed his Dublin ticket for one to London.

And rather than call and explain, Matthew had slunk home and demolished the best part of a bottle of whisky, planning on contacting her tomorrow.

Right now, she'd be looking at his terse text, wondering what on earth was going on with him. Much as he doubted his ability to explain while half drunk and via the useless method of communication available, he had to try.

Her cell switched to voicemail.

He didn't leave a message.

*****

The Coffee Haven stopped living up to its name a week later. In the middle of the mid-morning rush, when the line of customers desperate for their caffeine-fix stretched to infinity, April almost fell over when she looked up into a familiar pair of navy eyes.

"What can I get you?" With a huge effort of will she resisted the urge to add 'asshat'.

"You." Matthew's gaze was so intense it seemed to reach inside her and squeeze her insides.

"Americano? Cappuccino?"

"As you won't answer my calls, I've come to talk to you." Joshua glanced over. "Everything okay, April?"

She smiled at him. "Fine."

When she glanced back at Matthew, a muscle was pulsing in his jaw.

"I'd appreciate it if you'd give me your order." She glanced pointedly at the ever-growing queue. "We're busy, and I'm working."

"Cappuccino," he growled.

"Have here or takeaway?"

"Oh I'll be having it here. I'm not leaving before you talk to me."

"Move along please."

She fixed his cappuccino herself, adding a slightly different swirl motif on the top.

He stared at it.

"It's a J," she infused her tone with sugar. "For jerk."

His frown should have made her feel better. He looked terrible, with dark shadows under his eyes and his cheeks was definitely gaunt. She should be cheering at his misery. Instead, she just wished he'd leave.

With a precision honed from years of work, she deftly fixed all manner of coffee-laced concoctions for the long line of customers. Blocking him out was impossible. He perched on a stool near the serving area, ignoring his coffee, and watched her like a lion eyeing a mouse.

When everyone had been served, he walked up to the counter again. "Now, April."

She glanced over at Joshua. "I'll just be a minute."

He nodded, and took over.

She walked around the counter, and stood before Matthew. "I'm working, Matthew. This isn't convenient."

His mouth thinned into a tight line. He pushed a hand through his hair. "What time do you finish?"

"I don't have anything to say to you." She shoved her

hands into the front pocket of her apron.

"What time."

She drew in a ragged breath. He'd called her every day, and every day she'd bounced him to voicemail. This couldn't go on, she was a total wreck. Much as she didn't want to, they needed to have this conversation so she could put this whole episode behind her. "I finish at four."

He leaned in and pressed his lips to hers in a hard kiss that left her breathless, and then he turned and walked out.

"So, who's Mr. Intense?" Joshua asked when she returned behind the counter.

"He's someone I used to know." She really didn't want to talk to anyone about Matthew. Her body had reacted instantly at his nearness, she'd breathed in his distinctive scent when he'd leaned close. And to her eternal shame, she hadn't pushed him away when his mouth touched hers. "It's over."

Joshua's blond eyebrows rose. His grin made her wish she could have fallen in love with him rather than Matthew.

"It didn't look over."

She crossed her arms. "It's in the process of becoming over." Her heart clenched at the thought of never seeing Matthew again, after today. He obviously still wanted some sort of relationship, and once upon a time it would have been enough. But not now. Not when she dreamed about him every night, and wanted him with an urgency bordering on obsession.

What was always supposed to be a quick fling, a temporary affair, had changed forever. She didn't just want Matthew, she craved him. At the wedding, she'd let her mind roam down unfamiliar corridors. She'd fallen in love with Matthew. A man who didn't love her back.

It had to be over.

There was no sign of Matthew when her shift was done. She tossed her apron in the basket, and slipped her leather jacket on. His absence shouldn't have been a surprise, but it was. He'd seemed so determined...

He was waiting at the door to her apartment.

She walked past him, slid her key into the lock with a shaking hand, and stepped into the old iron elevator. He followed, sliding the lattice closed behind them.

She reached for the button, but his hand clasped hers before she could press it.

"April." He stepped so close his chest brushed against hers. His hands rested on her hips. There was no escaping him, nothing to focus on except him.

She was wearing flat pumps, so he towered over her. With every breath she breathed in his familiar scent. The touch of his large hands on her hips burned through her pleated black skirt.

She glanced up to meet his intense navy gaze that flicked between her mouth and her eyes.

"Don't..."

Too late.

His mouth lowered, claiming her lips in a masterful kiss. He backed her up to the wall of the lift, moved his hands to bracket her head as he traced the seam of her lips, demanding access.

The sensual assault shredded her defenses. Her body flooded with heat as his tongue brushed against the top of her mouth. Her chest was pressed against his, and her nipples tightened into tight buds beneath her silk bra.

I can't forgive him, I can't.

With a groan, April gave in to her body's urgings and slid her hands up his wide expanse of perfect chest, feeling the muscles flex beneath her fingers. His neck muscles were corded beneath her questing fingers.

He kissed with an urgency that was beyond sexy.

As her fingers slid into his hair, his mouth travelled down her neck. His hips rocked into hers, pressing a hard erection to the juncture of her thighs.

If I don't stop this, we'll be making love in the elevator.

The thought splashed over April like a bucket of cold water. She pushed at his chest. Jerked her head to the side. "Stop."

Matthew took a step away. His chest rose and fell rapidly with every breath.

Just looking at him hurt. She looked away, and pressed the button juddering the elevator into life.

He didn't speak until they were inside the apartment with the door closed.

"Do you want a drink?"

"No."

April strode into the kitchen and pulled an opened bottle of white wine from the fridge. He'd followed her in. She could feel his gaze on her back as she poured the pale liquid into a large goblet. She took a sip. Then turned, holding the glass before her like a shield.

"I should have come to the wedding."

"Yes. You should. You said you would."

"I know." He ran a hand through his hair. "I changed my ticket from Dublin to London at the last minute." He shoved his hands into the front pockets of his worn jeans.

"You could have called me." Anger rose like a wave. "I waited for you."

"I should have called." He stepped forward.

She stepped away. "I really don't want to get into this."

"You need to know the reason why."

"If I wanted to know, I would have answered your phone calls." Her hand clenched into a fist at her side. "I didn't. I don't. "

"You're going to hear anyway. I'm not leaving." He pulled out a chair and sat.

April puffed out a frustrated breath. "Fine." She sat across the table from him, like chess grandmasters engaged in a monumental battle.

Matthew's hands rested on the table. She stared at his knuckles. Those long fingers had gripped hers, had traced every inch of her body, over and over again.

"Going to the wedding would mean something to everyone there. They'd think I'd moved on from June, moved on to you."

Her gaze flickered up.

"What's between us is nobody's business."

"So you didn't want to make our affair public? Were you ashamed of being with me?"

His mouth twisted. His head shook in vehement denial. "I'm not ashamed of anything. I'm damn sick of having my motives analyzed by people who haven't given me the time of day for years. I don't need to prove anything to those people. I don't need their approval."

"I defended you." At least her voice didn't waver. "I told all my relatives you and I were together. I said you'd be there." She gritted her teeth. The day of the wedding had been bad enough, but the following morning…having to make a stupid excuse for his absence and seeing the pity in her family's eyes had been a lot worse. "You hadn't contacted me for days. I didn't even know where you were. Until you called for phone sex."

His eyes flashed blue fire. "I didn't call for phone sex."

Her brows rose.

"I called because I couldn't stop thinking about you. You've become an obsession I had to try and break."

"Why?" the word was dragged from her by a compulsion to understand. "What's so bad about…"

"Loving you?" he bit out. "You said it was lust. I can do lust. There's no expectations. There's no risk."

"You love me?" April's foolish heart fluttered.

"I damn well love you." His hands clenched into fists. His body was rigid with tension. "It makes me weak."

His declaration flowed through her body like a shot of some powerful drug. But his furrowed brow—the tense set of his shoulders—filled her with trepidation.

He met her gaze like a man before a firing squad, waiting for the hail of bullets.

April's heart pounded. Her mouth was dry and she felt lightheaded, as though she wasn't getting enough Oxygen.

She reached out and touched his hand. "What if I told you I love you too?"

Heat flashed in the depths of his eyes. "You don't have to say…"

She stood and walked around the table. Slipped between his parted thighs and the table. Rested her hands on his shoulders. "I love you. I hate what you did, but I love you."

He pulled her onto his lap, and kissed every other thought from her mind.

Chapter Fifteen

"This is decidedly gross." April wiggled her toes in the chilled water.

"Gross, but effective." Amy peered into the depths. "They're loving it."

The thought of tiny mouths nibbling at her feet made April queasy. The sensation was pleasant enough, a faint tickling on her soles, and apparently the benefits of a fish pedicure were well worth it so she tried to put the thought of tiny stomachs filled with dead skin from her mind.

"After this, we'll have a massage and a hot stone treatment." Amy leaned back on her outstretched arms a look of bliss on her face. "You can't believe how much I need pampering."

"How the heck did you end up in Guatemala anyway?"

Amy had been decidedly evasive about her latest trip since Matthew picked her up from the airport. In the past couple of days they'd talked about everything except Amy's latest adventure, and April was so curious she thought she might burst.

"There was a man involved."

"A gorgeous man?"

"Unfortunately."

Amy was as open as a blue sky, so her close-lipped response was puzzling. "Couldn't he help when your money was stolen?"

Amy's mouth turned up. "He stole it."

April's jaw dropped. "He…"

"Gorgeous but deadly. I thought…" She shook her head. "He's really not worth mentioning. Tell me more about the show tomorrow night. What are you wearing?"

April resolved to winkle the rest of this story out gradually. "I whipped up a little something." She'd sourced some fabulous fabric from her supplier and had created a new dress that was bound to blow Matthew's socks off.

"Black or white?"

"Shades of green."

"To go with your new hair. Good thinking, Batman."

The oft-used phrase from their teens made April smile. Red hair, green dress, was she channeling Poison Ivy or what?

*****

June didn't make the catwalk show. But her wedding dress did.

As a surprise, Michael had extended their two-week honeymoon to a month's cruise around the Caribbean, so the wedding dress had been sent to London brideless. Luckily, April had just the solution.

April stood backstage and gazed out at the darkened theatre. Large glistening chandeliers cast list onto the catwalk that stretched like a runway into the audience.

Marie waited her turn clad in June's shimmering wedding dress.

"If I fall over…" Her face was white. Her hands shook.

"You won't." April hugged Marie tight. "You'll be perfect." When June bailed at the last moment Marie had generously agreed to take her place.

It was almost time. "Now. Go!" April stepped back and watched Marie strut her stuff down the runway at the finale of the show. Her entire body fizzed as though it was filled with sparkling fireworks. The reaction to the show was electric. Already, her favorite designer had sought her out, mid-show, and asked if she would be interested in a job.

April had clutched the little white business card tight as she'd promised to call.

Marie reached the end of the catwalk, turned, and sashayed back.

April's heart was in her throat. The models clustered around her, ready for their final appearance before the crowd.

"April Leigh!" the compere shouted.

She linked arms with Marie and followed the models down the runway to the sound of applause.

Only the first row was visible from the stage. Amy, Eliza, her mother, father and Inez were all in the front row, cheering wildly. As was Matthew.

He stood and handed her a deep red rose as she drew level. Blew her a kiss.

The crowd went wild.

A balloon of happiness floated in her heart. In the past couple of weeks Matthew had met her friends. They'd travelled to Ireland, and spent time with her mother and his family. They were still living apart, but spent the nights together at her house or his apartment. His presence at her show was the icing on the cake. They might not be happy-ever-after, but they were certainly happy-for-now. They loved each other, she didn't need more.

*****

Everything was ready. Logan Advertising's team were ready at the start line with their monitoring equipment, which had been rigorously tested over the past week.

"Go." Jason pushed Matthew's arm. "We have it covered."

"Wish me luck." Jason knew of Matthew's plan for today.

"You won't need it. She'll love it." Jason grinned. "You're a brave man though. I wouldn't have the balls to do what you're going to do."

"Sure you would, for the right woman." What they had was almost perfect. They met up every evening for a run, and then after went to his house or her apartment to spend the evenings together. But it wasn't enough. Wasn't perfect. He wanted her to know the depth of his love. Wanted everyone to know. There was only one way to show her he was serious. Publicly.

The streets were packed with spandex-nistas. The air buzzed with estrogen as eager runners lined up ready for the off.

"I better go." Matthew searched the sidewalk for a way through. "The girls will be waiting."

A thumbs up from Jason, then he was cutting through the crowd to the staging post where the supporters stood, clutching signs before a bank of cameras.

Marie, Eliza and Amy jumped up and down as they saw him coming. Amy had slotted right back into April's life as if their time apart had never happened.

He walked right into the little group. "Are we ready?"
Wow, girls really do squee...

"I'm so excited!" Eliza gripped his arm so tight it almost cut off his blood supply. "She's going to love it."

"Nobody tipped her off?" He fixed each in turn with his give-it-up-glare.

"No way." Marie shook her head. "We wouldn't ruin this for anything."

"They're off!" Amy shouted. "Get ready!"

There was no way of seeing April in the crowd, no way to judge her reaction to what was to happen. Matthew's stomach clenched tight as he logged in to the race's URL and typed in the RFID tag number from the tiny device tied onto her shoelace tracking her position.

"She's left the starting grid."

Along the course, there were five mats which registered a runner's progress around the course. It shouldn't take long for her to pass over the next mat. Her time had increased substantially since they'd started training. If it hadn't been a women only event, he'd be right there running with her.

Spending each evening running, talking along the way was his second favorite way of getting hot and sweaty. Showering together after their run was fast becoming addictive.

Last week, she'd had her hair cut into face-framing layers, and tinted warm red.

She looked great with her hair any color, but red was fast becoming a favorite.

The emerald dress she'd worn at her fashion show made her look so hot he'd been gasping for air. She'd received so many compliments she was already gathering brightly colored fabric swatches for her next collection.

"Look." Amy pointed at the tablet. "She's pinged."

Matthew picked up the first sign.

Go, April Go!

She'd told him she loved his makeshift sign the first time around, so he'd had signs professionally produced with the words he wanted to say printed large.

He held it up in front of his chest, grinning like a fool as he imagined the effect seeing it would have.

*****

April's lungs burned as she rounded the corner. The last screen was just up ahead, and she couldn't wait to see what sign Matthew would be holding up when she reached it.

The steady rhythm she'd set since the start of the race meant her time would be more than respectable—the hours of training with Matthew had paid off big time. She'd never thought running would become such a satisfying pastime, in fact, she'd only started because Matthew loved it so much.

She liked sharing his passions. Loved the changes running had gifted her body. She'd always been lean, but honing her muscles had streamlined her look, and increased her stamina.

Stamina was good.

The first sign, "Go, April Go," had made her smile.

The second "I'm giving you a massage when we get home," had made her giggle.

The third "I love you," had brought a tear to her eyes, especially when she saw the look in Matthew's eyes.

He'd told the world.

Her pace picked up as she approached the sign.

The image of her friends and lover filled the screen. Amy, Eliza and Marie were jumping up and down; she could only imagine the sounds they were making by watching their mouths open and close.

Matthew stood dead center. His face was somber,

serious.

The moment she saw the sign she stopped dead and stared.

"I won't run. Will you?"

Emotion blindsided her as she fought for breath. She swiped a hand over her face, feeling the dampness of tears on her cheeks.

"No," she whispered. "No."

He waited at the finish line, with the sign at his feet.

"Help me out here," he muttered as she ran straight into his arms. "Say you won't run."

Her gaze tilted up to his. "Only to you."

Matthew pulled her close. He slipped a circlet of gold on her finger, sparkling diamonds and sapphire chips glinting in the sunlight.

"Eternity starts now."

Other books by Sally Clements

Catch Me A Catch
Bound to Love
Marrying Cade
The Morning After
Love On The Vine
Blaze
Challenging Andie
Angel All Year

For more info on upcoming releases, please check my
blog, www.sallyclements.blogspot.com
or contact me on twitter @sallywriter

Printed in Poland
by Amazon Fulfillment
Poland Sp. z o.o., Wrocław